SHE WAS BACK IN THE DARK STAIRWAY AT BELLECOURT—

Julius and his robed disciples filed up the dark stairs searching for her. She heard the sound of their relentless advancing footsteps echoing up the black corridor, the throb of the tom-tom drum, and the disturbing rattle of the calabash gourd. Desperately she tried to shut out the ominous beat, the wailing, chanting voices, but they sounded louder by the second. She had just realized there was no escape from her prison when she saw the serpent slither from the shadows toward her and she fell sobbing and screaming against the locked panel door.

"Sara . . . stop it!" Gentle hands were pulling her up, and Piers's voice was talking to her.

"Piers? We have to get away . . . they're coming." She struggled to get the words out.

Strong arms pressed her against his chest. "It's all right, Sara. Nothing will hurt you while I'm here. . . ."

Other SIGNET Books by Glenna Finley

- ☐ **BRIDAL AFFAIR** (#Q5962—95¢)
- ☐ **JOURNEY TO LOVE** (#T4324—75¢)
- ☐ **KISS A STRANGER** (#Q6175—95¢)
- ☐ **LOVE IN DANGER** (#Q6177—95¢)
- ☐ **LOVE'S HIDDEN FIRE** (#Q6171—95¢)
- ☐ **LOVE LIES NORTH** (#Q6017—95¢)
- ☐ **A PROMISING AFFAIR** (#Q5855—95¢)
- ☐ **THE ROMANTIC SPIRIT** (#Q5577—95¢)
- ☐ **SURRENDER MY LOVE** (#Q5736—95¢)
- ☐ **TREASURE OF THE HEART** (#Q6090—95¢)
- ☐ **WHEN LOVE SPEAKS** (#Q6181—95¢)

THE NEW AMERICAN LIBRARY, INC.,
P.O. Box 999, Bergenfield, New Jersey 07621

Please send me the SIGNET BOOKS I have checked above. I am enclosing $_____(check or money order—no currency or C.O.D.'s). Please include the list price plus 25¢ a copy to cover handling and mailing costs. (Prices and numbers are subject to change without notice.)

Name_____

Address_____

City_____ State_____ Zip Code_____

Allow at least 3 weeks for delivery

LOVE'S MAGIC SPELL

∞

by
Glenna Finley

Ⓞ
A SIGNET BOOK
NEW AMERICAN LIBRARY
TIMES MIRROR

Copyright © 1974 by Glenna Finley

All rights reserved

SIGNET TRADEMARK REG. U.S. PAT. OFF. AND FOREIGN COUNTRIES
REGISTERED TRADEMARK—MARCA REGISTRADA
HECHO EN CHICAGO, U.S.A.

SIGNET, SIGNET CLASSICS, MENTOR,
PLUME AND MERIDIAN BOOKS
are published by The New American Library, Inc.,
1301 Avenue of the Americas, New York, New York 10019

First Printing, August, 1974

1 2 3 4 5 6 7 8 9

PRINTED IN THE UNITED STATES OF AMERICA

I will a round unvarnish'd tale deliver
of my whole course of love; what charms,
what conjuration, and what mighty magic!

—Shakespeare

Love's
Magic Spell

Chapter One

Piers Lamont was turning into the drive of New Orleans' Municipal Station when he first observed the attractive brunette waiting near the curb. He bestowed a quick glance of approval as he drove by, deciding it was a pity that the mayor didn't plant more beautiful women on parking strips instead of bothering with palm trees. They might cost a little more, but the results were certainly worth it.

He noticed the young woman again when he'd parked his car and was striding into the station. A man would have to be dead not to take a second look at what the gods offered, he decided. And today the gods had excelled.

There was silky dark hair falling to her shoulders and delicate features spaced by a master hand. Not only that, her figure was beautifully proportioned even in a tweed suit determined to camouflage such things. Fortunately, the tweed skirt was the proper length to disclose a truly admirable pair of legs and ankles.

Piers grinned to himself as he noted the slight sheen of perspiration on her haughty nose as he passed by: probably she was wishing she could shed that suit for something more suitable to New Orleans' muggy seventy-degree noontime temperature. Visitors had to learn that November in the South bore little resemblance to the North's icy blasts. Then he promptly forgot her as he looked at his watch again and hurried toward the train platform. From the stragglers coming through the door, it looked as if the Chicago train had been on time for a change, and Stephanie would have his head if he missed meeting her precious guest.

Sara Nichols watched his disappearing back from under discreetly lowered lashes and sighed audibly. It would have been too much to hope that the Lafayette Motor Hotel would send such a good-looking man to meet its guests. Not that she approved of such masculine assurance, but she wasn't surprised by it. By the time any man with a tall, wiry frame like that reached his early thirties, he must be accustomed to encountering admiring feminine glances.

She sighed again and wished that she were dressed as sensibly as he. His dark green sport shirt and slacks looked superbly comfortable along with emphasizing his tanned skin and lean features. His hair was worn short and slicked crisply back, but the tone remained a defiant dark copper. Much more interesting than her own brunette color, she decided. Especially since the muggy Louisiana air was causing it to hang limply against her neck.

She looked at the empty taxi rank again and felt her temper rise. So much for New Orleans hospitality. If something with wheels didn't come along in five minutes . . .

There was still thirty seconds to go when Piers

came back through the station entrance. This time there was a frown marring his thin, intelligent face. The Panamá Limited had been standing on the tracks but the only people beside it were two porters discussing the last game of the New Orleans Saints. The passengers, they told him, had long since departed. Now he'd have to go back and admit to Stephanie that he'd neglected to retrieve S. H. Nichols until it was too late.

His glance once more slid over the young woman waiting at the curb, but it was the studied unhappiness on her quickly averted face that made him pause in mid-stride and detour her way. "Is there something I can do . . ." he started to ask and then his tone became curt as he saw her shoulders stiffen. "I wondered if you needed help."

"Thank you, no." Her voice matched the uncompromising set of her lips.

Piers felt a stab of irritation. My God! Obviously she thought he was trying to pick her up. So much for his Good Samaritan fling. "That's all right then," he said blandly. "I'm glad everything's under control. For a minute I thought you didn't understand that you have to phone for a taxi down here." He nodded formally and started to turn away.

"Just a minute . . . please." She had the grace to flush at his mocking expression when he swung back. "I didn't know . . . about having to call for a taxi. Would you mind terribly . . . I wouldn't bother you except that I've broken the heel on my shoe and I'd prefer not hobbling to the telephone." She waggled a slim foot, and Piers noted that the black pump encasing it was minus a heel.

"Why didn't you say something before now?" he began, only to have her interrupt impatiently.

"Because I didn't want to cause a fuss." She opened her purse and exhibited a shiny black heel in the palm of her hand. "Here's my evidence."

"I didn't doubt you for a minute. Where do you want to go?"

Her beautiful blue eyes turned frosty. "I can settle that with the cab driver. If you'd just telephone for me..."

He didn't bother to hide his annoyance either. "That's what I'm trying to do. The taxi company needs a destination when I call."

By that time, Sara felt as if her cheeks were on fire. Her blouse was glued to her shoulder blades under her tweed jacket and rivulets of perspiration dripped down her back. If she stayed much longer on the sunny sidewalk, she would simply dissolve into a blob on the cement. For a moment, she thought irrationally of walking to the hotel barefooted; it would be easier.

"Where are you staying in New Orleans?" Now he was enunciating between each word warily as if she didn't understand the English language. "You must have a record of it somewhere ... maybe if you looked in your purse."

"Oh, for heaven's sake ... I don't have to look in my purse. I know perfectly well where I'm staying. Or supposed to be staying. Since they didn't bother to pick me up ... I'm tempted to go somewhere else."

"Didn't bother to pick you up?" His thick eyebrows came together.

"That's right," she went on, "it's a place in the French Quarter called the Lafayette. The cab company must know the address." Her gaze sharpened as he stood staring down at her luggage. "Well, aren't you going to call?"

"S . . . H . . . N . . ." He was reading the initials on the black and white tweed cases aloud. "That couldn't stand for . . ."

"My name is Nichols. Although I don't see how it could possibly matter to you. Look, don't bother about the cab . . . I'll call myself."

He ignored her protest. "Did you just come in on the Panamá Limited?"

"Well, yes, but . . ."

"S. H. Nichols." His tone became accusing. "You're supposed to be a man. That's what they claimed at the hotel. No wonder I couldn't find you."

"I don't understand. Why should you be looking for me?" Her delicately arched brows climbed. "You mean—you're from the Lafayette?"

"That's right . . . Miss Nichols," he finished after noting the bare fourth finger of her left hand.

"You don't look like . . ."

". . . the man who collects young ladies at the railway station?" A grin slashed his tanned features as he picked up one of her suitcases. "I'm new at the job. You'd better wait here while I bring the wagon around. Otherwise it'll be dot and carry, with that missing heel." His grin widened. "If it were twenty degrees cooler, I'd offer to carry *you*."

"That's hardly necessary," she assured him, but she waited until he had strode toward the parking lot before rummaging for a handkerchief to wipe her forehead. She didn't even need her compact mirror to confirm that her nose was shiny, her lipstick needed renewing, and her hair was hanging in limp tendrils. When she added a tweed suit and a heelless shoe... she could only shake her head dismally.

Her bitter summation was interrupted by a late model station wagon pulling in to the curb in front of her. She watched her rescuer get out and come around to open the door on her side. Calmly, he stuffed her remaining luggage onto the back seat, leaving her no choice but to sit in the front beside him.

"Watch your head, Miss Nichols." He waited until she was safely inside before closing the door. Then, whistling cheerfully, he went back around to the driver's seat.

She noted a taxi turning into the station drive as they pulled out.

The man at her side jerked his head toward it, "It's a good thing I found you when I did. Stephanie would never have forgiven me if one of her guests showed up in a taxi."

Sara would have preferred the anonymity of a taxi—at least until she was looking human again—but she merely nodded and then asked, "Should I know who Stephanie is?"

"Not really. I've been a little remiss in the etiquette department." He half-turned to give her an amused look. "Stephanie Paige runs the Lafayette. Incidentally, I'm Piers Lamont."

She drew back like a wary kitten who had stuck

an unsuspecting paw on wet concrete. For a new employee, Piers Lamont was rushing his fences.

If he noticed her slight withdrawal, it wasn't evident. His next question couldn't have been more innocuous. "Have you been to New Orleans before, Miss Nichols?"

"No, this is my first time." She was intrigued by his pronunciation of "Noo Aaaleens." It was the first evidence of his southern forebearers. "Actually the city looks different from what I expected ... all traffic, industry, and skyscrapers." She gestured toward the imposing International Trade Mart building a few blocks away. "That's not as tall as the Sears Tower at home, but they're from the same fabric."

"I can tell you've been reading the tourist pamphlets on New Orleans." Piers slowed to let a truck make a left turn in front of him.

She flushed a little at his obvious amusement. "You mean, 'the city that care forgot' ..."

"Something like that. Don't sell us short in five minutes, Miss Nichols." He laid a deliberate emphasis on the last two words. "New Orleans refuses to be catalogued even by beautiful young northern ladies."

His left-handed compliment made Sara more aware of her disheveled state than ever. She managed a stiff smile. "Sorry, Mr. Lamont—I didn't mean to cast any slurs. Actually I've been anticipating this chance to see New Orleans. I just wish I had time to stay longer."

Piers didn't bother to exhibit even token curiosity about her itinerary. Instead he simply turned down a narrow one-way street, saying, "This is the start of the French Quarter or the Vieux Carré as most of the natives call it. There are some good examples of old iron grillwork on those balconies up there."

"Oh, they're beautiful!" Sara was enchanted with her first glimpse of the famed quarter with its crowded red brick buildings fronted by elaborate balconies and window grills. Occasionally she could glimpse a secluded inner patio through iron gates, but generally the tiny shops and boutiques pressed side by side without an inch to spare. The narrow sidewalks were occupied by strollers—a far cry from the busy pedestrians in most eastern cities. Sara mentioned the difference to Piers as he braked for a traffic light after inching through some hazardous intersections.

"That's because this is tourist territory," he told her with a faint smile. "Nobody hurries on a vacation. In the evening, Bourbon Street is turned into a pedestrian mall to make it easier for visitors to spend their money. Are you planning to enjoy the night life, Miss Nichols?"

"I . . . suppose so." Her brows drew together as she tried to think what she'd read about nightclubs on Bourbon Street. As she remembered, a flush surged under her cheekbones. "Er . . . probably not. I'm traveling alone . . ."

He accelerated carefully as the light changed. "You're quite safe on Bourbon Street if you *want* to be." There was no denying the amusement in his tone now. "On the other hand, you might enjoy it more with an escort."

LOVE'S MAGIC SPELL

There was a distinct silence. As it lengthened, Sara noted he made no attempt to volunteer his services.

To hide her mortification, she stared out the car window as if enthralled by the period charm of the old quarter, but her thoughts were on the man by her side. He knew very well that no woman would tour the risqué open-door nightclubs of Bourbon Street on her own if she had an option.

He spoke up finally, not bothering to hide his grin. "Of course, Stephanie could arrange something for you."

"That really won't be necessary..."

"I'd volunteer myself," he continued as if she hadn't spoken, "except that I don't even know your name. And a man can hardly take a woman out for dinner and call her Miss Nichols all night."

Her chin went up. "You're absolutely right. I couldn't put you through it." She allowed herself a fleeting glance at his profile before transferring her attention to the lean hands on the steering wheel. "Is it much farther to the Lafayette?"

"Practically no way at all." If he was disconcerted by her second direct snub, he didn't let on. "Just a few blocks down Chartres Street." He pronounced it "Charter" and looked amused at her bewildered expression when she saw a street sign. "Don't give it the French pronunciation," he advised, "or nobody will know what you're talking about. And don't ask me why. Incidentally, that's the Lafayette down there on the right." He nodded toward the next block. "The French Market's close by ... so's Jackson Square if you plan to sightsee."

"It sounds very nice," she said, sorry now that the ride was almost over. "Thank you for taking the scenic route." She kept her tone casual as they pulled up alongside the hotel office which was housed in a low brick building. "That's your job though, isn't it? Showing the guests around?"

He turned off the ignition and got out, coming courteously around the car to help her. "Not really, Miss Nichols. Come along into the office, and Stephanie will tuck you under her wing."

"But my bags . . ."

"George will take care of them." He indicated a grizzled black man who was heading toward them with a welcoming smile.

"Afternoon, Mr. Piers." He directed an appreciative glance toward Sara. "Ma'am."

"Afternoon, George." Piers caught hold of her elbow. "This is Miss Nichols . . . first time she's been to town."

The old man's head bobbed. "Afternoon, miss . . . welcome to New Orleans." He glossed over the name in the same soft way that Piers had earlier. "Miss Stephanie's waitin' inside for you."

"Thank you . . . George," Sara tried not to sound as bewildered as she felt and hobbled behind Piers as he pushed open a heavily carved door.

"You'll have to excuse the informality," he told her, "but I don't know George's last name. S'matter of fact, I don't think he knows mine. First names are an old southern custom . . ." Then, before she could answer, he led her over to a counter at one end of the paneled room where a blond woman slightly older than Sara was waiting for them.

A gentle frown creased her forehead as they approached. "Piers, for heaven's sake—didn't you find Mr. Nichols? I promised Colonel Sherman that we'd roll out the red carpet . . . now he'll be furious."

"Stop fussing, Steff . . . this *is* Miss Nichols. You and the Colonel had your sexes mixed."

"Well, you *are* a surprise," Stephanie said, leaning on the counter and bestowing a sweet smile on Sara. "Welcome to New Orleans, Miss Nichols."

"Thank you—I'm happy to be here." As she replied, Sara took another look at Stephanie Paige's kind, interested features and decided that she liked what she saw. Perhaps her nose was a little long, her chin a little short, and the pale blue eyes dreamed in a heart-shaped face, but she possessed a mane of glorious strawberry-blond hair which overcame all of the other shortcomings. She wore it pulled back from her face and secured casually with a tortoise-shell barrette. Her clothes were equally casual; a denim skirt with a matching denim jacket over a pale blue blouse. As she came around the end of the counter, Sara saw she was bare-legged and wearing a pair of blue canvas oxfords.

The way she put a proprietary hand on Piers' wrist as he lounged against the wall indicated they were old friends as well as being in the same age bracket. "Piers honey, you just about saved my life. I'd plain forgotten about George having the morning off. Did you ever find time for lunch?"

"Nope, but it's good for my waistline to skip it once in a while."

"At least share some coffee with me." She gave his arm an impulsive squeeze. "We can have it in the patio just as soon as I get Miss Nichols settled. How does that sound?"

"Like just what I've been waiting for. I'll wait outside for you." He pulled up as he reached for the doorknob. "Perhaps Miss Nichols would join us?"

"I ate on the train, thanks." Sara didn't explain that she'd merely breakfasted on the train. If Stephanie Paige wanted to eat lunch with her new employee —and she obviously was looking forward to it—that was her business. "I'll just register and go on up to my room."

"Whatever you say," he said casually before closing the door behind him.

Stephanie smiled apologetically and became businesslike once again. "If you'll just sign the card . . . Thanks, that's fine. Here's your key. . . . Your room is in the main wing on the second floor."

Sara started to take the key and then realized she was still clutching the heel from her shoe. Quickly she unzipped her purse and stuffed it inside, before accepting the key. "Thank you. I should be a little more presentable after a shower. Frankly I didn't realize that it was so warm down here in November."

"You're lucky just now. Last week it was raining buckets," Stephanie said with a native's candor. "Look . . . why don't you join us for coffee. Colonel Sherman is an old friend of ours, so it would be nice to get acquainted."

"That's kind of you, but I think I'd better clean up a bit," Sara said hastily, determined not to be an awkward third at the table. Then, feeling she'd better set the record straight, "I should explain that

I've never met Colonel Sherman ... he's just a business acquaintance of my aunt's."

"That's all right," Stephanie said. "Actually he just thought you might need someone to watch out for you while you were in New Orleans, but we can discuss it later." She was frowning as she went over and peered through the glass door at the back of the office. "Now where do you suppose George got to? I'd take you up myself except that somebody has to stay near this darned switchboard. This is our slack time or there'd be more staff around," she went on in explanation.

"If you'll just point me in the right direction, I can find it by myself."

Stephanie gave her a relieved smile. "No problem there. Go outside and take the stairs to your right. Your room overlooks the central patio and pool. I'll make sure that your bags are sent up as soon as I find that rascal George."

"The only thing I really need is another pair of shoes," Sara said, reaching for the doorknob. "Thanks for sending your driver down to meet me at the station. Will the charge be on my bill, or should I have paid him personally?"

"Meeting guests is a complimentary service of the hotel. I'm just sorry you were kept waiting."

"Then maybe I should have tipped Mr. Lamont."

Stephanie's laughter bubbled forth. "I wish you had ... I'd love to have seen Piers' face." Then, meeting Sara's puzzled glance. "Honey, didn't you know? Piers doesn't work for the Lafayette."

Sara resisted an impulse to rest her forehead against the cool glass panes in the door and counted to five slowly instead. Only then did she manage to say, "I don't think I understand."

Stephanie's amusement faded as she noted the other's genuine distress. "I sent an SOS to Piers this morning when I found that George wouldn't be available. Somehow, it didn't seem friendly just to have a taxi driver meet you—" She broke off at Sara's expression. "Is something wrong?"

The younger woman was trying to remember exactly how rude she'd been in snubbing Piers Lamont's overtures on the drive from the station. It was a wonder that she hadn't jibbed at sharing the front seat with him. She'd done everything else.

"Do you feel all right, honey?" Stephanie's concern was evident. "You'd better sit down for a while. Louisiana humidity can be terrible when you're not used to it."

Sara took a deep breath. "I'm fine, thanks. It's just that I remembered something I'd forgotten." Then, realizing that her explanation wasn't making any more sense than her behavior, she tried again. "I'll just go on up to my room. Later on, I'll get your advice about sight-seeing. Thanks again for all your help, Miss Paige."

"Stephanie, please..."

"Stephanie, then." Sara agreed, opening the door. "See you later."

"Right. Remember, top of the stairs and then right. And the pool's officially open... if that's more appealing than a shower."

Sara nodded and hobbled toward the stairs. Inwardly she was deciding to stick with the shower. In her present mood, the deep end of the swimming pool could be a temptation, especially if Piers Lamont walked by.

As it happened, he wasn't at the poolside. He was leaning against the door of her room, taking care to stay under the shady eave of the roof as he watched her approach. That way, he was able to enjoy the panoply of emotions chasing across her features when she discovered him.

"What in the dickens are you doing here?" she asked, keeping a wary distance.

"Just bringing your bags, ma'am."

"*Must* you talk like an old southern retainer?" She pushed her hair back with a defiant gesture. "I'm surprised you aren't carrying a tray of mint juleps as well—or is that Kentucky instead of Louisiana?"

"You've been out in the sun too long," he said calmly before reaching over to pluck the key from her fingers. He unlocked the door and waved her inside.

Still in a daze, she stood and watched him bring in the bags with an economy of movement, before closing the door behind him and opening the blinds. The whir of the air conditioner could barely be heard but she was aware of refreshing cool air surrounding her, and as light flooded the room, she was able to appreciate the furnishings. "Oh, this is lovely!"

It was clear that he expected the comment. "Stephanie thought you'd appreciate this room. The hotel won a Vieux Carré Restoration Honor Award last year for its decorating." His lazy nod encompassed the canopied rosewood bed with its stark white crocheted bedspread, the faded red brick walls which were stripped of ornamentation, and the sheer white drapery hangings at the windows. A deep blue rug covered the planked oak floor both in the bedroom and in the tiny sitting area where a circular rosewood table was flanked by two slipper chairs upholstered in blue-and-white velvet.

"It certainly isn't furnished like any hotel room I've ever been in," Sara said faintly. She watched his slow grin as he hoisted her bags on two needlepoint luggage racks. "But then, I've been wrong about everything since I arrived. You could have told me you weren't the regular hotel driver," she added angrily as he started to chuckle, "so there's no use dragging the joke out and waiting for a tip. Just close the door when you leave . . ." Her voice faltered on the last words despite her efforts to keep it steady.

"Hey, take it easy," he frowned suddenly. "I didn't know you were going to take this seriously. What's happened to your sense of humor, Miss Nichols?"

"*Will* you stop calling me Miss Nichols?"

"I'd like to," he flared back. "If you hadn't been so damned hidebound about etiquette, we'd be sitting down to lunch in Brennan's patio now instead of still circling at arm's length like a couple of new kids at school. What in the hell *does* S. H. stand for, Miss Nichols?"

"Sara Halliday . . ." she murmured, completely taken aback by his outburst.

"Sara . . ." he drawled the name experimentally, giving the vowels an easy southern treatment that she'd never heard before. "It suits you." He strolled over to the door. "You know my name. What time shall I pick you up for dinner?"

"Dinner?" She sank down on the side of the bed because there suddenly wasn't any strength in her knees.

"That's right. How about seven thirty? You look as if you could use some time to pull yourself together," he added with brotherly candor. "I'll call from downstairs so you won't have to wait around."

Her chin came up at his casual assumption she'd be standing on the curbside again. "Now look here, Mr. Lamont . . ." At his pained look she started over, "Look here, Piers Lamont . . . I don't even know you. What makes you think that all you have to do is whistle and I'll come running?"

He moved back beside the bed and stood laughing down at her. "No—you look, Sara Nichols . . . you can spend all afternoon finding out about me. Ask Stephanie. Or call Colonel Sherman if that isn't enough." His gray eyes warmed as she dropped her glance in confusion. "But you know damned well it isn't necessary, my girl." His finger came up to trace her delicate cheekbone and then teasingly flicked the end of her nose. "You want to go out to dinner with me just as much as I want to take you. Call it a *lagniappe* of New Orleans if you need to soothe your conscience." He swung back to the door and waited by it for confirmation.

Sara opened her mouth to protest, then closed it again. Piers was right—she had every intention of going out to dinner with him. The prospect was making her heart scud along like an America's Cup contender even now. What's more, she had no intention of checking his credentials with either Stephanie or Colonel Sherman. The only thing she *did* want to ask was what a *lagniappe* was. But when she saw the mounting impatience in his glance, she decided that could wait a while, too.

"Seven thirty, Sara?" He had the door half open. "Best bib and tucker."

"Seven thirty," she confirmed faintly to the carved door as it closed firmly behind him.

When his call came from the lobby that evening exactly at the appointed time, Sara felt that she was in better shape to cope.

A leisurely bubble bath had helped—along with tea and sandwiches served in her room. Afterward she had flipped a mental coin to decide between sight-seeing and a short nap on her comfortable canopied bed. Since she'd had little rest on the train the night before, the nap won—and she fell asleep almost immediately. The sound of voices from the poolside eventually woke her and she was surprised to find that it was already after six. By the time she'd changed into a silver evening skirt with a magenta-and-silver striped top of the same material, she was beginning to feel better. And when she'd spent an inordinate amount of time combing her hair and smoothing on a touch of soft blue eyeshadow, her comfortable feeling had changed to one of pure anticipation. After answering the phone, she was able to assure Piers that she'd be right down and then deliberately spent two more minutes applying a last stroke of cherry lipstick so that she wouldn't appear too anxious. Finally she spoiled the whole effect by catching up her silver evening sweater and purse and hurrying along the balcony toward the stairs. She saw Piers' tall figure come to the top of the stairway and tried to slow to a dignified saunter before he noticed.

His sudden grin told her that she didn't succeed. "There's no hurry," he drawled, reaching out to take her glittering sweater and drop it over her shoulders. Then he stepped back and raked her with a masculine glance that caused Sara's pulse to pound even harder. He whistled soundlessly. "For you—I'd have waited."

The tone of his voice made Sara decide it would be safer to bring things under control immediately or they'd never make dinner. She smiled over her shoulder at him as she started down the stairs. "I hope you noticed that this time I come complete with shoes *and* heels. I thought you'd appreciate the change."

"Very nice." He caught her elbow at the bottom of the stairs and steered her toward the street. "There's a cab waiting. It's easier than trying to find a parking space around here."

She nodded and watched as he went ahead to open the car door for her when they reached the sidewalk. Tonight he'd exchanged his sport shirt and slacks for a well-cut dark suit worn with a pale blue shirt and foulard tie. His hair was slicked down again, but part of the thick thatch fell over his forehead as he bent forward to help her in the car. His fingers shoved it back impatiently before he slid on the seat beside her. Evidently Piers wasn't a man who bothered with careful masculine hair stylings, and Sara found herself chalking up another mark to his credit.

"What's the matter?" He was watching from his corner of the seat. "You look as if you'd just discovered a wolf in the haystack instead of Little Boy Blue."

She brought her attention back with an effort. "Sorry ... I didn't mean to."

"Good." He rubbed a thumb along his jaw line. "For a minute, I thought I'd missed some place shaving."

"Of course not." Sara kept her voice matter-of-fact. "You look very nice ..."

"Good lord, girl ... I'm not fishing for compliments." His well-shaped eyebrows drew together. "Relax. We're just going out for dinner, and I've been warned to stay on my good behavior, so you don't have to look as if you're booked for the next shipment to Siberia."

"What do you mean ... you were warned?" she asked, ignoring the latter part of his sentence. "Are you serious?"

"Absolutely." He leaned toward her slightly as the cab driver increased his speed once they were clear of the French Quarter's narrow streets. "Both Stephanie and Colonel Sherman insisted that I wear kid gloves handling you. In fact, it was all I could do to convince the Colonel that he was not the man who came to dinner. He can hardly wait for tomorrow to strew rose petals in your path." Piers' eyes were narrowed with amusement. "I didn't know when I was angling for a date that you were such valuable merchandise. What hold do you have on the old gentleman?"

"Why didn't you ask Stephanie?" Sara asked, not pleased that she had been so thoroughly dissected.

"Because I'm asking you." Then, before she could answer, he reached for his wallet saying, "Never mind. We can settle it over dinner. That's more civilized than haggling in a taxi."

"I had no intention of haggling ... as you call it." She broke off as the cab drew to a stop under a hotel marquee. "Is this where we're eating?"

"That's right ... the Pontchartrain. The food's good and it's not quite so crowded as the places in the Quarter." He was out of the cab and helping her onto the sidewalk as he spoke. "I think you'll approve."

"Ummm, yes," she agreed as they went through the small lobby and up a short flight of steps to an impressive dining room.

An attentive maître d' apparently knew Piers well because he greeted him by name and immediately ushered him to a corner table which was sheltered from the others by a walnut planter box.

"Enjoy your dinner, Mr. Lamont ... Madame." He bowed when they had been seated, summoning a waiter for their drink order.

Piers didn't bother with the menu. "What sounds good, Sara? An old standby or something more southern—like a Sazerac?"

"What's in that?"

"Whiskey and abisante. It used to be absinthe in the old days."

"Help!" She shook her head hastily. "That's too lethal for me."

Piers grinned. "A champagne cocktail? That's safe and sane."

Sara nodded, determined that she wouldn't take more than a token sip of anything. She was having enough trouble keeping a rein on her senses even cold sober.

"I hope you don't mind that I've already ordered," Piers was saying as the drink waiter disappeared.

"Not unless you've included fried catfish. I saw *that* on the menu at the Lafayette when I called room service this afternoon."

"You didn't try it?"

She merely shook her head.

"Poor Stephanie." He sighed with amusement. "She's determined to push the local dishes, but her guests won't cooperate. I can recommend her chef's gumbo, though. You'll find variations of *that* all over town." He leaned back in his chair as the waiter put their drinks in front of them.

Sara nodded her thanks and nibbled on the piece of orange decorating her glass. "My aunt told me that the important thing about gumbo was never to ask what was in the bottom of the bowl. Aunt Prue's the reason I'm in New Orleans."

"Prue?"

"Prudence Nichols. She's my aunt by marriage." She looked up to find his lips twitching. "What's so funny about that?"

He made an effort to sound serious. "I was just thinking how appropriate her name was ... under the circumstances. Sure she isn't a blood relative?

Your behavior at the station was thoroughly in keeping."

Sara smiled ruefully. "Aunt Prue would have been laughing her head off if she'd seen me. From a shy little southern girl, she's systematically worked her way through three husbands. The last one—my Uncle James—died, but she's still on the best of terms with the other two."

"And she's responsible for your being here?" Piers' tone was politely probing.

"That's right." Either the sips of champagne had helped or Sara was getting accustomed to his presence across the table. "I might as well tell you all about it. If I don't, you'll just ask Colonel Sherman."

"Probably." There was no rancor in his tone. "I understand she inherited a plantation."

Sara nodded. "Some huge old thing called Bellecourt."

"A very beautiful 'huge old thing,'" he corrected and watched her smooth complexion flush at the gentle reproof. "You'll agree when you see the place."

Sara's lips firmed. "Right now my aunt needs an abandoned plantation the way she needs three Great Danes in her apartment. It's a pity she broke her ankle last week or she would have come down here herself."

Piers ignored her stiff tone. "Broke her ankle, eh? That's too bad. How did it happen?"

"She fell over the third Great Dane pup when they were both trying to answer the telephone." Sara smiled reluctantly as he chuckled. "I feel guilty because I chose that pup for her in a mad moment. So when Aunt Prue said that she couldn't sell Bellecourt without someone in the family taking a last look at it, I had to volunteer. But don't expect me to change any plans," she added hastily. "Aunt Prue's bank account is healthy, but she can't afford to restore any plantations. I understand those projects run into the millions."

"That depends on the size of the mansion," he said judiciously.

"From what Aunt Prue said, Bellecourt comes in a large economy size which she can't afford." Sara pulled her sweater more firmly around her shoulders. "I wish you wouldn't make me sound like Mrs. Scrooge at the orphans' picnic."

"Believe me, I didn't mean to. Your aunt is lucky to have such a conscientious guardian," he said.

"Good heavens, I'm not her keeper. Aunt Prue admits she's impulsive and she likes the family to help out at times. My father has an import business so he's usually traveling away from home. That means I'm the one who has the job of keeping her solvent." Sara smiled. "The last time Aunt Prue dabbled in real estate it was a hunting lodge on an island in northern Minnesota. She wanted me to inspect it in the middle of winter."

"Cold?"

"Absolutely perishing. It was like that old W. C. Fields' joke—'I spent a week there one night' . . ." Her lips curved in remembrance. "Would you believe that I was waiting on a pier for the boat back to the mainland three hours before it was due?"

He chuckled appreciatively. "Well, at least you'll fare better on the weather here."

"It's wonderful!" she admitted. Then she leaned forward, resting her forearms on the table. "Honestly, I don't mean to give you the wrong impression. I love Aunt Prue. Dad and I need her just as much as she needs us." She broke off, suddenly embarrassed by her catalogue of family affairs. "Sorry, I didn't mean to bore you."

"You didn't—"

She broke into his denial deliberately. "What about your family? Have you lived in New Orleans long?"

"Long enough." He took a swallow of his drink and swirled the ice absently. "My great-great grandmother caused a furor by marrying one of the 'Kaintuk Americans'."

"What was so strange about that?"

"It wasn't done in those days. She was part of the French colony . . . and the two elements didn't mix. Canal Street divided the Americans from the Creoles then."

Sara spoke her thoughts aloud. "A French grandmother accounts for the 'Piers,' doesn't it? Isn't it French for Peter?"

He grinned reluctantly. "Go to the head of the class. Fortunately, all branches of the family are speaking to each other by now, but it took a couple of generations to do it."

Sara was wondering how she could ask if that included a "Mrs. Piers" when she was saved the trouble.

"These days my sister and I are the only ones left.

Her husband's from Michigan and thinks family trees are the silliest damn things he's ever heard of. I'm inclined to agree with him, but it's safer not to mention the topic around people like Stephanie and the Colonel. They're the backbone of the State Historical Society."

"Don't tell me they're still fighting the War between the States . . ."

He leaned forward to put his glass on the table. "Not exactly, but people down here feel strongly about their heritage and talk about it more than other parts of the country."

"It's easy to see you haven't been in Virginia lately," she said, her eyes twinkling. "But joking aside, I have the feeling that I'm being furnished a copy of the house rules before I see Colonel Sherman and Bellecourt."

"Something like that," he admitted. "I'm putting it badly."

"Not at all." She was well aware that he was handling it very competently. Piers was obviously an experienced campaigner when dealing with women, however much he denied it. "It's strange you should be so interested in Bellecourt," she mused. "From your speech, I wouldn't even know you were a southerner. At least most of the time."

"I haven't spent much time here since college."

"Umm, I gathered you don't make a career out of meeting people at the New Orleans station," she said dryly.

"I didn't know what I was missing. I may be a permanent fixture there from now on." He grinned at her reproving glance. "On my off days, I work in sugar."

"You're speaking to a woman who only knows that it comes granulated, powdered, or in cocktail cubes."

"I'm surprised you didn't just say brown and white," he admitted. "There's a little more to it than that. For the last couple of years, I've been helping set up some mills over in Swaziland. The Africans learn from us and we learn from them," he added cryptically.

"What will you do next?"

"I'm trying to decide between signing a new contract abroad or working here at home for a change." His tone lightened. "I don't plan to make any hasty decisions; I can pick up pretty girls waiting at the station for a month or so."

"Sounds like fun." She hid her disappointment at his casual pronouncement. "Too bad I won't have any spare time. Colonel Sherman wants to get down to business tomorrow."

"Then we'll just have to celebrate thoroughly tonight, won't we?" Piers picked up his fork as the waiter put down the plates for their first course. "I hope you like crab cocktail."

His uncaring attitude made Sara feel she'd choke on the first bite. Then she managed a careless smile to match his. "It's one of my favorite things ... and this looks delicious!"

Later, she didn't find it difficult to exclaim over the rest of the dinner. It would have been a strange woman who didn't enjoy an icy hearts of palm salad,

Tournedos de Boeuf, and later, the Pontchartrain's towering ice cream pie served with chickory coffee.

All through the meal, both she and Piers followed an unspoken agreement to keep the conversation on impersonal subjects. New Orleans weather was explored to the fullest, being treated with a solemnity that would have been funny at any other time. After that, they discovered a mutual liking for winter vacations, pro football, and colonial furniture, which saw them safely through dessert. Then Piers politely inquired if she wouldn't like to sit in on the jazz concert at Preservation Hall later. Sarah shook her head.

"No, thanks," she said, barely able to hide her relief that the interlude was over. "Colonel Sherman is coming fairly early to drive me to Bellecourt—so I'd better not be late tonight."

"Whatever you say." Piers frowned for the first time when he signaled for the check. "You're probably tired."

"Not really ... I had a nap this afternoon," she started to say before remembering her part. In her confusion, she dropped her napkin and by the time she had retrieved it, she had her lines firmly in order. "Actually I am a little weary. It's the reaction after getting ready for a trip. You know, the packing and all ..."

"Maybe you should have some hot milk before you go to bed," he said skeptically, letting her know that the trip between Chicago and New Orleans didn't exhaust many of his acquaintances. "Is Colonel Sherman driving you directly to Bellecourt?"

"I suppose so." His query stopped her in the middle of pushing back her chair. "Why shouldn't he?"

Piers put down a tip and pushed the salver away. "No reason. He's a hospitable soul, so he probably plans to show you around the countryside. He owns a small plantation near Bellecourt. Actually he's your nearest neighbor."

Sara's eyebrows went up. "I didn't know that ... although he could have told Aunt Prue. Maybe that's why he wants her to sell Bellecourt. Does he need the extra land? For his business, I mean."

"Damned if I know. You'll have to ask him." Piers wasn't giving anything away. "The Colonel has a thriving real estate business in Jefferson ... that's the nearest town to Bellecourt. Maybe Lee could use the extra acreage."

Sara found herself wishing that he would discard his impersonal tone. "Who's Lee?" she asked, not really caring.

"Lee Sherman ... the Colonel's son. He's a cane farmer and they never have enough land. If you really want to know, we could go over and ask him."

"I don't understand."

"He's having dinner over there." He nodded toward the end of the room. "That table for two next to the wall ... with the good-looking blonde in blue."

As Sara turned to look, she was conscious that his impersonal tone had warmed when he described the blonde. Too much so for an unknown acquaintance. Her expression became thoughtful as she located the woman he had mentioned. There was no doubt that she was a stunning, statuesque creature, but Sara was equally impressed with her escort's good looks. He was a rangy fair-haired man in his late twenties wearing a well-cut dinner jacket in midnight blue with a pale blue shirt. His sun-bleached hair was worn just above collar level but brushed back from his tanned aquiline features. As Sara stared, he put his napkin on the table and got to his feet, waiting cheerfully for his partner to join him.

"It looks as if they're leaving," Piers put in laconically. "Do you want me to bring them over to be introduced?"

"Oh, no." It was with some difficulty that Sara tore her gaze from Lee Sherman's tall form as he escorted his dinner companion from the room. She noted that their passage resembled a royal procession, complete with bowing waiters and an obsequious maître d'.

Piers had been watching as well. "That attention isn't all for Lee," he pointed out. "Mary Lou owns a good hunk of real estate around town including a couple of office buildings."

"Mary Lou being the 'good-looking blonde,' " Sara quoted, with a bite in her words.

"That's right." Piers pushed back his chair. "They've known each other for several years. Lee doesn't let his cane plantation interfere with his social life ... as you'll undoubtedly find out," he added carelessly as he stood up. "The Colonel will probably introduce you to his son and heir tomorrow. Incidentally, you'll enjoy seeing their house. They have some armoires that half the women in the Historical Society would mortgage their souls to own." Without giving her a chance to reply, he motioned her ahead of him.

Sara found their exit greatly resembled that of Lee Sherman and his companion. Maybe *everyone* was given such deference when they dined out in New Orleans, she thought. And then as she intercepted some of the warm feminine glances cast at Piers, she realized credit should be given where it was due. "Do you know *everyone* in New Orleans?" she asked eventually when they were waiting for a cab at the curb.

"Hardly. My sister has a lot of acquaintances in town. You'll have to meet her . . . if you have time," he added, politely helping her into the cab. "Stephanie can arrange it. They went to school together."

Sara kept her distance on the rear seat and looked straight ahead. "I doubt if there'll be time. If I'm leaving tomorrow . . ."

". . . and going to bed early tonight," he filled in without expression. "Then don't count on it. Tell me, Miss Nichols," he put a casual hand on her knee, "did you bring that frost all the way from Lake Michigan?"

Startled, she jerked around to face him. "I don't know what you mean."

"The hell you don't." He kept his voice low so the driver couldn't hear. "You've been acting like a polite zombie for the last half hour. Right now you're wondering if you'll make it back to the Lafayette with that maidenly virtue of yours still intact. Well, you can relax, Sara." He patted her knee once before pointedly removing his hand. "My victims have to be willing. Southern gentlemen have an aversion to screaming females. And we never handle the merchandise..."

"... when you're just window shopping," she finished for him. He raised his eyebrows in reproof but she was too angry to notice. "Well, I'm sorry not to offer my services but no doubt you have plenty of volunteers."

"Absolutely." His voice was bland. "Once the line was so long somebody thought they were waiting for tickets to the Sugar Bowl."

She flounced on the seat, aware now that the driver was blatantly eavesdropping *and* enjoying it. "Maybe you should see a psychiatrist about that imagination of yours. You've either stayed in the African sun too long or it's the humidity down here. Anyhow, you can forget about that hot milk therapy—I'd suggest a cold shower in your case."

"Well, what do you know! Ruffled feathers, after all." He gave a short laugh. "I didn't think it was possible." His hand shot out to close on her wrist and pull her toward him. "Let's make that cold shower worthwhile."

Unfortunately just then the cab slowed to a stop in front of the Lafayette. Sara yanked her hand away as the driver reluctantly got out to open the door.

Piers was watching her closely. "We'll never know what would have happened. You *should* be relieved," he said.

She was aware that she wasn't relieved. Instead she was suffering from a sensation of deprivation and she had the feeling that Piers knew it.

Consequently, her voice was sharper than usual.

"So should you. Now your record of willing victims is still intact. Goodnight, Mr. Lamont."

"Hey . . . just a minute . . ."

She shook her head, realizing that if she stayed around any longer she'd lose the last vestige of poise. Clutching her sweater around her shoulders she fled around the end of the office building and up the iron stairway.

It wasn't until she was unlocking the door of her room that she realized that she hadn't even thanked him for dinner. For an instant she debated painfully before her good manners overcame her reluctance. She should at least attempt to acknowledge his hospitality. Slowly she retraced her footsteps along the balcony, hoping unconsciously that he would have disappeared by the time she reached the courtyard.

As she neared the stairs, the murmur of voices from the patio below made her stop and peer through a planter box of greenery on the railing. She had no desire to make her apologies in front of strangers, as well.

Below her, two figures moved from the shadows into the subdued lighting near the pool. Piers had his arm companionably around Stephanie's shoulder and was laughing softly at something she had just said. Sometime during the evening the southern woman had changed from her casual daytime attire to a black floor-length chiffon gown with an extravagant skirt that flowed like gossamer as she moved. Sara noted that it also provided a perfect foil for her blond hair which gleamed under the light of a patio torch.

"Piers honey, be serious for a minute," she was

murmuring. "How much do you think she knows? I thought you'd learn *something*."

"Not a chance. From now on, I'll be the last to find out anything." His voice rose distinctly in the quiet night air. Only the soft splash of a small waterfall at the far end of the pool competed with their conversation. "Miss Nichols couldn't wait to get rid of me. You'll have to do your own sleuthing from now on, honey. I must have lost my touch while I was overseas."

Stephanie gave a tiny crow of laughter. "Don't tell me the mighty Piers finally struck out?" She moved closer to curve an arm around his neck. "Tell me all about it . . ."

Sara didn't wait to hear any more or watch Piers bend to Stephanie's willing lips. She *did* manage to tiptoe back along the balcony, but once she reached the safety of her room, her temper erupted like a Cape Canaveral missile.

To think that Stephanie Paige had arranged the entire evening! And to think that she'd been idiotic enough to care what Piers Lamont felt. Worrying about her lapse of manners when he was merely satisfying his curiosity all along.

Sara pulled out a pair of pajamas and slammed her suitcase lid back down so hard it bounced. So much for southern men and their "gentlemanly" reputations! At least she'd gotten across the idea that she thoroughly disliked him. Frowning, she remembered belatedly that he had commented on it quite cheerfully.

Then she defiantly tossed her pajamas over her shoulder and moved toward the bathroom, concluding that she certainly wouldn't lose any sleep over the situation. Piers and Stephanie could bill and coo all night if they wanted to.

After that rational assessment, it was especially aggravating to find herself still wide awake at three A.M. By then, she was completely exhausted and had collected a nagging headache as well. When her travel clock showed three thirty, she finally got up and rummaged in her purse for two aspirin, grimacing as she swallowed some tepid water with them before padding back to bed.

Apparently Piers was right again—she should have ordered that damned hot milk.

Chapter Two

Colonel Sherman was a southern gentleman of the old school. He gallantly ignored the dark circles under Sara's eyes when he collected her for the trip to Bellecourt the next morning and beamed as if her presence made his day worthwhile.

"I'm terribly sorry that I couldn't meet you at the train yesterday," he told her, tucking her into the front seat of a battered station wagon. "Some rental contracts needed to be signed at the last minute so I had to call Stephanie for the rescue. She tells me that Piers Lamont finally found you at the station. Mighty kind of him—" He broke off as George came around the office carrying Sara's luggage. "Half a minute ... I'll unlock the rear door," the Colonel instructed him. "We'll be on our way in two shakes," he assured Sara over his shoulder.

She nodded and watched him start to supervise the storing of her luggage before she slid farther along the seat. Obviously the Colonel was a stickler for doing things properly.

From her glimpse of his son the night before she had expected to meet an elderly soul complete with white linen vest, a broad-brimmed hat, and a sugared accent. Instead Colonel Sherman was a vigorous, fit-looking man in his late fifties whose only concession to age was a thinning thatch of white hair brushed back from a high forehead. Otherwise his tanned skin was firm, and his sharp blue eyes didn't miss a thing. There was a decisive quality to both his speech and gestures which indicated he was used to having his own way. While he wasn't as tall as his son, anything further from the legendary "Kaintucky" colonel wedded to his rocking chair would be hard to find.

When he had seen her luggage installed to his satisfaction, he slipped a bill in George's jacket pocket, gave him a genial nod, and came around to settle on the driver's seat beside Sara. "That takes care of everything, I think," he remarked with satisfaction. "Now we'll be on our way."

He drove swiftly and competently through the crowded streets of the French Quarter until he turned onto a busy thoroughfare which led directly to a freeway arching its way northward from the city limits toward Baton Rouge. The still waters of Lake Pontchartrain stretched along the highway to the right for as far as they could see.

Sara found the unfamiliar terrain of special interest. "I didn't realize that there was so much water around New Orleans," she commented as the miles went past.

The Colonel nodded somewhat grimly. "Oh yes, that excess of water has caused trouble all through history. Imagine a saucer with New Orleans in the center and the waters of the Mississippi on a level with the edges—then you'll understand the trouble we've had."

"But aren't there levees?"

"Of course, and spillways too, these days." He turned to smile at her reassuringly. "Things are under control most of the time. You'll see the levee when we turn off onto the River Road in a few miles. That's where the big industry is, as well."

"I was wondering," Sara said, looking out at the lakeshore again. "It's hard to imagine a more peaceful place than this. There isn't any comparison with Lake Michigan." She gestured toward the periphery of Lake Pontchartrain which was crowded only with vegetation. Water hyacinths grew rampant in one shallow sector where the shore line was fringed with pine trees whose roots were obscured by dark green palmettos. Spanish moss draped the branches of the trees looking like somber widows' weeds above the metallic gray cast of the water. Occasionally there would be a cluster of shallow-draft dinghies at ancient docks—a far cry from modern marinas on the Great Lakes. The fishing huts which supplied bait and groceries were a casual appendage to the docks, and they, too, looked like an illustration from other days with their planked porches, birdhouses hollowed from yellow gourds, and iridescent dragonflies winging through the balmy air. Long-legged white birds completed the picture, gliding overhead in slow swoops timed to the tempo of life below.

"*Now* I know where they got that saying . . . 'the place that care forgot,'" Sara said. "I thought they just meant the City of New Orleans."

"Not any more," the Colonel admitted. "At least

not the part of town that visitors inhabit. Did Piers take you sight-seeing yesterday?"

Her relaxed expression vanished. Why did everything have to lead back to the mention of Piers Lamont, she wondered bitterly. "There wasn't time," she replied. "We just had dinner together."

"Great Scott, you should have told me. I would have given you this forenoon to do some looking around."

"There wasn't any need. Actually I just came down to see Bellecourt and report to my aunt."

He pursed his lips thoughtfully. "I suppose you're right. Anyway, you can stop off in New Orleans on your way home. Stephanie and Piers will be glad to tour you about."

Sara's chin went up and she kept back an angry retort with a distinct effort. "There's no need for them to bother. I'll do my sight-seeing on another trip."

That time her tone was so stiff that he shot her a surprised glance before concentrating on his driving again. "Whatever you say. It's just that they both know the history of the area ..." his voice trailed off. When she didn't reply, he tried again. "At least, I hope you'll let me or Lee show you around the upcountry part of the state near Bellecourt. There are one or two plantations that are worth seeing. Of course, they're a great deal smaller than your aunt's inheritance. I don't suppose she has any thoughts of restoring her property?"

"Like the good old days?" Her tone softened as she noticed the restrained eagerness on his features. Like a faithful dog still hopeful for a walk even as the door closes. "Sorry, I'm afraid not. Aunt Prue cherishes her girlhood memories but she simply can't afford any projects like that. Too bad she didn't inherit a few oil wells along with the estate."

He nodded. "Unfortunately Bellecourt is mostly surrounded by swampland. It's the wrong part of the state to hope for anything else. My son found that out the hard way ... that's why he's raising cane on our place. Sugarcane, that is," he labored for the feeble joke.

She smiled politely. "I heard about that. Do you feel that's the best solution for Bellecourt—selling the acreage for cane fields?"

"As far as I can see." He broke off to say, "This is where we leave the freeway and turn north on the River Road. In a few more miles you'll see the levee and one of the plantations that's been restored. You might recognize it—they shot a television movie there a year or so ago."

Sara sat up straighter on the seat. "Perhaps Aunt Prue's property could be used like that."

"Now wait a minute! Don't start counting your chickens until you see Bellecourt. The folks in Hollywood want restored property for their epics ... not old mansions that are rotting away."

She winced at his frankness. "I didn't know it was that bad."

"Sorry, Miss Nichols. I didn't mean to be so outspoken, but there's no use getting your hopes up. It's just too bad that Bellecourt was allowed to fall into its present shape. The former heirs always hoped they'd come into a windfall so they could restore it, but the day never came. Half the folks

LOVE'S MAGIC SPELL 41

who own these plantations have been waiting for years to do the same thing. Those who farm sugarcane always hope for the coming harvest. Some of the owners actually go without enough food so they can pay the taxes on their places in the meantime. It's a crying shame."

"I didn't realize the big houses were such white elephants."

"They weren't always. Not in the old days when incomes weren't taxed and the planters had unlimited slave labor for field work." He slackened speed as they came up behind an immense tractor-drawn hopper piled to overflowing with lengths of sugarcane. Waving a hand toward it, he said, "These days if the ranchers didn't have mechanical cutters, they couldn't even afford to harvest the crop." He paused until he had passed the slow-moving vehicle before adding, "That lot's on the way to the refinery now. I suppose Piers gave you the background on the finishing process."

"Not really. He just mentioned that he was thinking of taking a job at home." She was casting about for a change of subject when the Colonel solved the problem.

"That's the river levee there to the left." He waved toward a steep grass bank near the edge of the road which wound endlessly ahead of them.

"But you can't even *see* the Mississippi . . . just the dirt bank."

"That's the whole idea. If water was coming over the top, we'd be making tracks elsewhere." He smiled reminiscently. "This levee is quite a sight during the Christmas holidays. The residents light tremendous bonfires on the top of the bank on Christmas Eve. You can see the pyres for miles."

"It sounds like fun."

He nodded. "Now—look over to the right. That shows what can be done after an expensive restoration." He let the car idle so Sara could stare at the magnificent plantation mansion set back from the road in a bower of live oak trees. "One of those oaks is over two hundred years old with a trunk that measures twenty-five feet around," the Colonel continued proudly. "You'll notice the architecture of the building is classic Greek Revival."

Sara's attention moved from the main house to the two smaller hexagonal buildings on either side of it. Their graceful curving roofs led up to a sharp point, bearing a resemblance to French chateaux in the valley of the Loire.

"Those are called *garconnières*," the Colonel explained. "You'll find them near many of the southern plantations. In the old days they were used for visitors who'd traveled long distances by horseback or riverboat and had to stay the night. Sometimes the *garconnières* were used by the young men of the family when the plantation families were large and bedroom space was at a premium."

Sara nodded and sank back against the seat as he accelerated and left the plantation behind. "I've never understood why the southerners adopted the Greek style," she said. "What did the architecture of the Acropolis have in common with Louisiana life?"

"Climate for one thing. The wide galleries gave protection from the hot sun. Actually our oldest planter homes were copied from the West Indies; the Greek style was adapted later by southerners who'd seen it done in England. The first styles were austere; the furbelows and fretwork of Steamboat Gothic came afterward." The dryness in his voice showed his distaste for this development.

Sara tried not to smile. "I hope I'll have time to see some of them."

"We'll have coffee at my place. It's a small house," he explained. "One of the West Indian single-storied structures with the wide porch. Quite a decent restoration—" he broke off, sounding almost shy. "Well, we'll wait and see what you think. Afterward, I'll arrange for you to tour Bellecourt."

Sara started to demur, wishing momentarily that she could tour her aunt's home by herself before remembering that she had to be practical. Without her own car, there wasn't any way to achieve this. She should be thankful that Colonel Sherman was taking an interest in her visit.

Another hour passed in pleasant, idle conversation before he turned from the highway into a narrow dirt drive which wound past a grove of live oak trees. The dull-green Spanish moss clinging to their lower branches brushed against the windshield making Sara feel as if they'd entered a secret garden cloistered from the modern world. Banks of rhododendrons and azaleas screened the daylight and when Sara rolled down her car window, she caught the fragrance of sweet olive in the air.

"I have a hard time remembering this is November," she confessed. "It's so warm that I expect to find everything in bloom."

"Too bad you couldn't have come in the spring. There are lots of visitors who make it an annual pilgrimage."

The drive turned into a cul-de-sac in front of a white house whose paint gleamed in the sunlight. A German pointer rose from his resting place under a magnolia tree and advanced toward them, tail wagging gently.

The Colonel stopped the car and turned off the ignition. Then he got out and bent down to stroke the dog's head. Sara came around to watch the exchange of affection.

"What a nice disposition he has," she said.

The Colonel grinned. "Lee and I bought him for a hunting dog. First trick he learned was to retrieve a flower blossom and present it to any visitor who came calling."

Sara's laughter bubbled. "A *real* southern gentleman."

"All I can say is that it's a good thing most folks are friendly." He urged her toward the wide porch steps. "I don't know about you but I could certainly use some coffee."

"It sounds wonderful to me, too." She pulled to a stop inside the screen door and surveyed the wide foyer with interest. A living room furnished with antique furniture opened on the left while a door standing partially ajar on the opposite side revealed a bedroom with a towering mahogany tester bed.

Just then, the same man Sara had seen the night before at the Hotel Pontchartrain emerged from a door at the rear of the hall. He had discarded the dinner jacket for beige riding breeches and a well-tailored twill shirt which was unbuttoned at the throat. His brown riding boots gleamed with polish and shattered the quiet as he marched toward them across the hardwood floor.

The Colonel's face warmed with affection. "Lee! I didn't expect to find you home in the middle of the morning." He drew Sara up beside him. "This is Miss Nichols ... Sara Nichols. She's come from Chicago to inspect Bellecourt for her aunt."

A slow grin wandered over Lee's handsome features as he captured her hand. "How do you do, Sara. My ESP must be working overtime today. Something told me I should go home for coffee." His clasp tightened. "This is much nicer than standing in the mud and seeing if the cane trucks are on schedule."

From the looks of his boots, Sara decided that Lee hadn't done much standing in the mud that morning ... or any other. His easygoing manner displayed more than a touch of insouciance which wasn't surprising. With his combination of tanned skin against sun-bleached fair hair, Lee could have been a rousing success selling anything to women ... on television or anywhere else for that matter.

The Colonel didn't appear to notice anything unusual in his son's presence. "Sara's interested in plantation furnishings," he told him. "Maybe you could show her some of our treasures while I order the coffee."

"Sure ... glad to." Lee shoved one hand in the front pocket of his breeches as he lounged against the door frame. "While you're about it, Dad, you'd better phone your office. Your secretary called about five minutes ago. She has some sort of a flap on."

Colonel Sherman's mouth hardened. "I don't know why I put up with that woman!" He broke off and turned to Sara. "Sorry, my dear. I'll try not to be long."

"Take your time," Lee cut in with a grin. "If I run out of 'treasures,' there's lots of other things we can talk about."

His father started to remonstrate and then merely shook his head before disappearing into the back of the house.

"Now then, Miss Nichols," Lee's deep voice was an open mockery as he gestured her into the living room ahead of him. "Do you want the good tour or the 'once over lightly' version before we get down to more important things?"

"Such as?" she asked demurely.

"Like how long you're going to be in Louisiana and what you're doing for dinner tomorrow night?"

She ticked off her fingers in turn. "Obviously not long enough, and I'd better wait and see, thank you." For a moment, she thought of mentioning that she had seen him at dinner the night before and then decided against it. There was no reason to bring Piers into the conversation if she could avoid it. Instead she let her eyes roam appreciatively over the rich furnishings of the room. "Seriously, I'd love to hear about your furniture. What's that beautiful thing?" She indicated a graceful walnut piece near the doorway.

Lee's eyes gleamed with mischief, but he obediently moved over to the table in question and took on the cadences of a professional guide. "Here, madam, you see a magnificent example of an early petticoat serving table. Designed and constructed by Millard or one of the other furniture geniuses, the table boasts a mirror on the lower part so that ladies could check the length of their petticoats as they passed by." Then he pointed to a gleaming cut-glass piece atop the table and directed a teasing look at Sara. "Since you're a northern lady, I'll bet you don't know what this is for."

She moved over beside him and inspected the rounded dish which was slightly larger than a covered cheese dish with a removable glass decanter top. "You're right," she finally confessed, rubbing a finger down over the curved glass sides. "I've never seen one before. What is it?"

He shot her a triumphant glance. "That, Madam Nichols, is a very practical thing; a genuine flycatcher. No household should be without one."

"A flycatcher!" Sara broke into incredulous laughter. "I don't believe it."

"You would if you could see it work. First of all, you remove the stopper—like this. Then you rub something sweet and sticky on the inside of the neck. Afterward just replace the stopper and put it on the dining room table at mealtimes. The flies crawl up under the rounded sides of the bottle but the curved edge prevents their escaping the same way. Notice that the bottom has sanded glass. That was done so Victorian ladies didn't have to offend their sensibilities by looking at the trapped flies during dinner."

Sara stared at it, bemused. "I'll be darned. I've never even seen one for sale in antique stores."

"That's because southerners regard their flycatchers in the same way that Bostonian ladies regard their hats." Lee kept his face solemn. "We don't buy them . . . we *have* them."

"Wouldn't you know! Now I'm panting to take one home with me."

Lee appeared to consider carefully. "Panting, eh? I always like to deal with beautiful women when they're desperate."

Sara raised her eyebrows. "Eager . . . yes. Desperate . . . no. I'd hate to give you any false ideas. Besides, I might find a lovely flycatcher at Bellecourt."

He shouted with laughter. "Not a chance, honey. There isn't anything left inside the old place that doesn't weigh a ton. All the rest was hocked long ago. Julius will tell you that." At her puzzled look, he said, "Julius is the caretaker. Didn't you know about him?"

She shook her head.

"He's been around the place for a million years or so. Well, at least ten," Lee temporized. "Originally he was hired as a gardener. Then when the staff dwindled and eventually disappeared, he stayed on as a caretaker. Sometimes with a salary; part of the time without."

"It's strange that my aunt didn't mention him. I'll bet that she hasn't a clue about a caretaker on the place. Good heavens, I wonder how much back salary he has coming."

"Well, don't worry about it. You can bet your bottom dollar that Julius isn't. He'd work for nothing if he could stay at Bellecourt. By now, he probably thinks it belongs to him. When he isn't tending his vegetable garden, he's busy trying to shore up the house." Lee thumbed a metal paper knife which rested on a small desk. "Of course, it's a wasted effort. Putting Bellecourt back in shape without enough money is like trying to remodel Windsor Castle on a small home loan. It's just a good thing for your aunt that the land around the house has some value."

His unfeeling appraisal of the property annoyed Sara. "I'll be interested to see Bellecourt," she pointed out. "My aunt has some wonderful childhood memories of the place, so she wants to be sure she's right in selling it."

Lee must have realized that he'd gone too far. His good-looking features softened with remorse. "Sorry, Sara ... I didn't mean to sound callous, but I've seen so many people down here commit financial suicide with their inheritances that it makes me mad. They talk about the sacred cows of India ... well, plantations come in the same category to southerners. It's not that Dad and I don't give a damn about old things." He gestured around the living room with its wealth of antiquity. "You can see where his extra money goes—but at least he doesn't attempt the impossible like old Julius."

Sara nodded slowly, acknowledging the truth in his argument. Actually he was saying the same things she'd told her aunt before coming south. "I know you're right," she began, only to have a knock on the front door interrupt her.

"Now who can *that* be?" Lee said irritably. "Delia's busy in the kitchen so I'd better go and see. Back in a minute," he added over his shoulder as he headed for the foyer, sliding the living room door closed behind him.

She heard the sound of the front door opening and then the murmur of masculine voices before the living room panel was pushed aside again and Piers strolled in with Lee on his heels.

" 'Morning, Sara," Piers' greeting was offhand. "I told Lee that we already knew each other so he could stop trying to keep me out on the veranda."

"That's exactly why I wanted to keep you there," Lee told him flatly. "You know plenty of women without latching on to visitors, too." He turned to Sara. "Why didn't you tell me that you'd met this interloper?"

She managed a wide-eyed stare. "Was it important? I didn't think so."

Piers winced at her frankness and Lee chuckled happily. "That puts you in your place, my friend," he told Piers. "I guess you're entitled to a cup of coffee, after all."

"Did I say something wrong?" Sara kept her innocent expression. "All I meant was that we'd just met yesterday. Piers is a friend of Stephanie Paige."

"Which is just the way we'll keep it," Lee said. He frowned then and looked at his watch. "I wonder what's keeping Dad? At this rate it'll be time for lunch before we get that coffee. Not that I want to hurry you along, old chum," he told Piers with a grin.

"Of course not." Piers sat down on a velvet-upholstered walnut settee with every evidence that he intended to stay a while. "If you want to check on the coffee, Sara and I can manage on our own. We can always talk about the weather . . ."

"And Stephanie," she added, tightening her lips.

"And Stephanie," he agreed.

Lee's grin widened but he moved over to the sliding door. "I guess it's safe. Keep an eye on her, Piers—she's fallen in love with that flycatcher of ours and you know how collectors are!"

"No holds barred," Sara replied. "I can see I'll have to try another approach." Her pleasant expression held until the door slid closed behind him and then her eyes turned frosty as they surveyed Piers' lounging figure. "What in the dickens are you doing here?"

This time, the wide-eyed stare was his. "Calling in on my friend Lee, of course. I didn't know that I needed permission. There's no need for you to be nervous—I never ravish a female before lunch. Very bad for the digestion." He settled himself more comfortably against the settee. "You can just figure my arrival's a little *lagniappe* for your day."

Sara forgot her disdain. "I meant to ask you last night. What does that expression mean?"

"*Lagniappe?* A little something extra. You could call it an added attraction."

"Well, your arrival hardly fits in *that* category." She strolled over to stand by a bank of windows which overlooked the porch. "You'd be amazed how well I've gotten along without you today."

"Really? From the circles under your eyes, I thought you were pining away. You look as if you *need* that coffee."

She stepped back, appalled at his perception. "I

don't need anything. Except a little peace and quiet."

"You're too young to be talking like that. What's wrong with your social life at home? You can't have had much experience with the opposite sex if you're upset by the slightest thing." His glance flicked over her. "You're old enough to know better, too."

"I'm twenty-four. You don't have to make it sound like ninety!"

"There you go again! I don't know why you're so sensitive," he added with masculine complacency. "I can give you nine years and it doesn't bother me."

Sara felt like reminding him that women didn't look at age in exactly the same way. She wouldn't have admitted, though, that he was the first man who'd made her feel as if she were going to be left high and dry on the spinster shelf.

His mocking voice broke into her thoughts. "Once you get some sleep, you'll feel better. That's all that's wrong with you." He broke off to yawn mightily. "My God, now you've got *me* doing it."

The opening of the sliding door forestalled Sara's angry reply. Lee came in carrying a trayful of coffee things, closely followed by his father. "Sorry to have taken so long," Lee said, putting the tray down on a walnut sideboard and starting to pour the coffee. "We wouldn't have blamed you if you'd taken off for the nearest hot dog stand."

"But we're glad you didn't," the Colonel said. "Piers ... it's good to see you." He went over to shake hands. "I heard you were back. How was Africa?"

"It'll never replace New Orleans. I thought I'd

drop in and pay my respects. Didn't know you had company." Piers' amused glance brushed Sara's as he made the last remark. Annoyed color flared in her cheeks at his obvious falsehood, but Colonel Sherman evidently saw nothing amiss.

"Sara isn't company. She's a friend of the family," he insisted gallantly. "But now something has to come along and spoil the first morning I could entertain a beautiful young lady," he added.

Lee passed Sara a steaming cup of coffee. "What Dad means is that he's been summoned back to the office for an hour or so. I offered to take over the guide duties—"

"But Lee's due back at the mill," the Colonel cut in with amazing firmness. "Harvest time is full of problems for cane people. Do you mind if we drop you at the guest house at Arcady for now? That's where you'll be staying for the next day or so. I'll try to finish my business and show you over Bellecourt this afternoon."

Sara frowned slightly, wondering why her tour of the plantation had to be arranged like visiting royalty. Surely she could hire a car herself.

Colonel Sherman seemed to glimpse the way her thoughts were running. "I'd like to be along on your first visit to show you the boundaries of the property and introduce you to Julius. The old man's a little difficult to deal with."

She nodded, deciding that his reasoning made sense. Later on, she could make her own arrangements. "All right, whatever you say, Colonel Sherman." She took a hasty sip of coffee. "You probably want to get going."

"My dear girl, don't scald yourself on that coffee. I'm not in that big a hurry."

Piers turned from the sideboard where he'd been helping himself to cream and sugar. "You might as well put me to work, Colonel. I'm on the way to Arcady myself for a few days—I'll be glad to drop Miss Nichols. That way, you and Lee won't have to bother."

Lee put his cup and saucer down on the coffee table with more force than was absolutely necessary. "I'll be damned! A year in Africa hasn't changed you at all, Piers. You always could manage to be in the front row when there was a pretty girl around."

Piers grinned and took a swallow of coffee. "Don't be a dog-in-the-manger. I'll bet you've already made a date with Sara."

Lee gave him a mocking glance. "Dinner tomorrow night, if you must know. And I don't intend to postpone it for any damned mill business," he told his father with some emphasis.

The Colonel ignored the challenge. "Then everything has been taken care of," he said in an even tone which encompassed all of them. "I'll pick up Sara this afternoon at Arcady. Incidentally, your room reservation is all taken care of," he told her. "I think you'll like the Inn. They serve the finest food in this part of the country."

"That's not surprising since Stephanie Paige has a hand in it. She's good at her job, I'm told," Lee said as he moved toward the door. He paused with his hand on it. "You still seeing as much of her as you used to, Piers?"

Colonel Sherman cut in before the other could reply. "That's really none of your affair, Lee. You'd better get along to the mill—I told them you were on your way."

Lee stood stubbornly for a minute, looking as if he'd like to argue. Then he turned to Sara and shrugged elaborately as if to say, "What can you expect from the older generation?" Aloud, he said, "Okay, Dad, I'm on my way. Sara . . . I'll phone you to fix a time for our date." His glance passed over Piers' quiet figure. "I reckon I'll be seeing you, cousin."

"Reckon you will."

As Piers calmly took another swallow of coffee, Lee turned on his heel and strode from the room.

Colonel Sherman put his empty cup on the tray. "I hate to run—but I'll have to. Piers, you're sure you don't mind dropping Sara at the Inn?"

"My pleasure."

"Then I'll be on my way. Have a good lunch, Sara . . . it's all right to call you Sara, isn't it? I can't let Lee and Piers upstage me on this." His eyes gleamed with amusement. In that instant, Sara could see where Lee had inherited his charm.

"Of course. I wouldn't answer to anything else," she assured him.

"Till this afternoon, then." He nodded and patted her shoulder as he headed for the door. "Take care of her, Piers. I won't forget this favor."

There was a silence in the living room after the closing thud of the front door.

"I feel like a parcel that's been delivered to the wrong address," Sara confessed finally, moving over to put her empty coffee cup on the tray. "I suppose it's silly to mention a taxi."

"Not even worth talking about," Piers confirmed. "Don't worry. You aren't beholden ... I *was* on my way to Arcady." He noticed her slight hesitation as they moved toward the front door. "What's the matter? You're getting that hangdog look again."

"If you must know—I'm disappointed," she said crossly. "I was all set to see Bellecourt this morning. Maybe that's being childish, but I've been looking forward to it for days."

He closed the door behind them and escorted her down the porch steps before saying, "To be honest, I had every intention of stopping by. I'd like to see the place again myself but I didn't see any point in telling the Colonel. Now we both have the perfect excuse—you decided to humor me and I'm merely bowing to your wishes." He pulled up beside the station wagon and opened the door. "We'll still get to Arcady in time for lunch."

Since he was being so obliging, Sara decided she'd better remain discreetly silent about the conversation she'd overheard the night before. Therefore, it came as a surprise a little later when Piers was easing the car through the winding drive to have him ask casually, "Why did you run away last night?"

Sara was surprised into an honest answer. "I felt that I was getting in over my head ... and it seemed the easiest way out. Actually I wanted to apologize—later."

He made an impatient gesture. "I'm not talking about the taxi. Why did you disappear from the balcony?"

She turned to face him, her jaw slack with surprise. "You mean you saw me?"

"Of course I did. And I heard you scuttle off, too ... like somebody who'd wandered into the men's locker room by mistake."

"That isn't funny. Obviously you and Stephanie didn't need or want any company."

"So *that* was it." For some reason, he sounded pleased at her weak response.

Sara darted a puzzled glance his way. "Part of it," she admitted. Then, "What did she want to know about me? Good lord, I don't have any state secrets."

"If you'd listened long enough, you'd know I told her precisely that."

"Oh, I listened," her sarcasm was evident, "but you weren't admitting much. At least until you kissed her. I didn't wait around after that."

Apparently a guilty conscience wasn't part of Piers' makeup. He merely grinned. "If you'd stuck around a while, you'd have seen that I was more kissed than kissing. Don't tell me a peck on the cheek puts me in Purgatory?"

"Was that all that happened?" Sara stopped abruptly. There was no point in admitting how shaken she'd been by that embrace.

Piers tactfully changed the subject. "As for my sleuthing, you'll have to ask Stephanie yourself. There'll be plenty of opportunity ... she'll be at Arcady for a few days, as well."

"But why? I thought her job was in New Orleans?" Even now, Sara wasn't sure that she wanted to see any more of the woman.

"The Arcady Inn and the Lafayette are owned by the same people. Stephanie divides her time between the two places."

"That's quite a coincidence, isn't it?"

"*Now* who's looking for trouble," he chided.

Sara subsided in the seat and gazed thoughtfully out the window as he turned back onto the main road. This time, though, the silence between them was comfortable and she was able to let down her guard. The leisurely drive through the warm air of the lush countryside was a needed tonic. By now, the reaction to her first day in New Orleans and the night virtually without sleep was making itself felt.

Piers must have been watching the gradual relaxing of her taut figure. "I'd like to tell you to curl up and take a nap but there isn't time," he said. "Bellecourt's just a hoot and a holler from here."

She struggled upright. "I don't want to miss anything." Her eyes narrowed thoughtfully. "I thought we'd left the river. When did we start following the levee again?"

"A little way back. You're never very far from it ... it winds all over the place. Did the Colonel show you the industrial plants on the shores?"

"Outside New Orleans?" She nodded. "I had no idea there were so many. For a minute, it seemed like the steel empires on the shores of Lake Michigan."

"Well, it's a change from the sleepy old days when Louisiana just raised cotton and indigo."

She half-turned in the seat. "I never thought of indigo being a crop. I just thought it was a color."

"Nope. It was harvested regularly, but not any

more. Nowadays," he indicated the fenced land at the side of the road, "it's cattle and cane."

"Well, despite all the industry, you'd never mistake this for the heart of Times Square." She smiled as she gestured toward a ramshackle building they were passing which proclaimed itself the Boll Weevil Café. It shared an intersection with the Creole Belle Grocery and an attractive grove of china-ball trees.

Piers chuckled. "You can take the people out of the South, but you can't take the South out of the people . . . thank God." The car slowed to turn onto a dirt lane. "A couple minutes more and you'll think you've stepped back in time. Bellecourt may have disintegrated inside but the outside . . ." he let his words trail as he pulled up to a high wrought-iron gate and shut off the ignition. Then he gestured toward a building looming impressively beyond a planting of magnificent oak trees.

"That's Bellecourt?" Sara's voice was a mere whisper.

He nodded again.

"Good heavens, it's the most beautiful thing I've ever seen," Sara murmured. She was scarcely conscious of speaking; all her thoughts were on the stately plantation home which gleamed whitely in the sunlight. Just as resplendent were the gardens, overgrown with neglect, but still a veritable paradise of color. Tremendous groves of rhododendrons and azaleas were interspersed with sprawling rose hedges whose runners stretched into unkempt clusters of grass. Underneath the oaks, beds of geraniums and marigolds flourished even in abandon.

The two-story mansion was built in a huge square

with eight magnificent columns to a side. Each column appeared to be at least four feet in circumference and thirty feet tall. At the second level, an immense outside gallery ringed the house to provide access to the upper story.

"Remember, they didn't waste space with hallways when it was built," Piers said, following her gaze. "The outside gallery provided access to the various rooms as well as ventilation. You'll find them on almost all of the old houses."

"This isn't a house—it's a legend." She got out of the car and waited for him to join her by the gate. "I thought Colonel Sherman said the estate was in terrible shape."

"He's right," Piers said soberly. "The inside has been gradually gutted over the years; Julius spends all his time keeping the exterior looking passable."

Sara opened her mouth to reply and then closed it again. It had been on the tip of her tongue to ask how he knew so much about the condition of Bellecourt since he'd been out of the country. Then she realized that he could have heard from a number of sources ... Stephanie being the most likely.

Piers didn't notice anything unusual in her silence. He was pushing ajar one side of the old gate and motioning for Sara to precede him. Passing through, she saw a wooden sign which hung drunkenly from the hinge. "Private Property—Absolutely No Visitors!" she murmured, "I hope Julius doesn't shoot first and ask questions afterward. Maybe that's why Colonel Sherman wanted me to wait."

Piers closed the gate behind them and urged her along the lane. "Don't be so pessimistic ... things look pretty peaceful to me." He jerked a thumb toward some chickens pecking their way along the edge of the lane. Nearby a tortoise-shell cat lay sleeping atop a tree stump in a patch of sunshine. Other than the sound of their footsteps on the turf, the buzz of an occasional fly was the only disturbance in air which had turned from balmy to just plain muggy.

Sara searched for her handkerchief to blot her forehead, aware that her nose must be gleaming by now and wishing that she'd done some restoration herself before leaving the car.

As they neared the house, Piers glanced around with a slight frown. "I thought Julius would have appeared before this. He usually has built-in radar where visitors are concerned."

"You mean he greets them at the gate?"

"Generally he makes sure that they don't get *beyond* the gate. The old fellow's held the fort so long that he doesn't like company."

She paused as they came to a path across the grass leading to the front entrance of the mansion. "But if the interior of the house has been stripped, where does Julius live? Surely he doesn't try to exist in there without any electricity or anything?" She waved toward the deserted building which looked more awesome than ever at close hand.

"Hardly. Even Julius isn't *that* dedicated. He's fixed up some outbuildings hidden in the trees at the back of the property. They're not too bad. He has a vegetable garden . . ."

"And chickens," she added dryly as an energetic white hen strutted past.

"... and chickens," Piers confirmed smiling. Then his features sobered as he said, "Look, I'd better try to find the old fellow before we traipse through the house. God knows what kind of repairs are needed by now—the back stairway was rotting out ten years ago. Why don't you sit down on the front steps and wait for me. Julius can't be far away—he never leaves the grounds."

"All right." Sara stifled an impulse to ask if she might go with him. There wasn't any reason to feel nervous about sitting on porch steps in the bright sunshine, even if there was an abandoned house behind them. She gave herself a mental shake and forced a smile. "Go ahead. I'll sit here and commune with the chickens."

"Good. I won't be a minute." Piers lingered long enough to say casually, "I wouldn't wander around if I were you."

Sara stared at him. "Why? Because I might fall through the floor or something?"

"Uh-huh." He sounded relieved. "Although, to be strictly honest, the downstairs floor took the count five years ago. It's down to dirt now."

She tilted her head to survey him. "You're remarkably well informed about a place that doesn't allow visitors. Do you have a crystal ball or did you subscribe to a weekly newsletter from Julius?"

Piers merely scratched the side of his nose. "Southerners are notorious busybodies. By tomorrow, everybody at Arcady will know whether you like grits for breakfast, how you stand on civil rights, and what kind of lingerie you favor." He gave her a casual nod. "I'll be back in two shakes."

LOVE'S MAGIC SPELL

She was watching his tall form disappear on a path that led around Bellecourt before she could think of a suitable answer. Or mention that he had ignored her questions again. Finally she smiled reluctantly and strolled along the path to the broad front steps. Then she stood and stared at the house in front of her in bemused silence.

She wasn't given to flights of fancy but she would have been completely devoid of feeling to ignore the aura of history hanging over the old mansion. It was still magnificent, she decided, even with its sagging porch, peeling paint, and facade of seedy neglect.

The minutes wore on. Sara stood irresolutely on the shallow steps, shifting from one foot to another. Finally she glanced at her watch, wondering why the search for Julius was taking Piers so long. By this time, he should have had time to cover all of the plantation grounds.

She looked again at Bellecourt's big front door, noting the oversized brass fixtures dull with tarnish. Her lips clamped in a stubborn line as her impatience mounted. Why, she asked herself, did she have to stand outside of Aunt Prue's inheritance and wait for an unknown caretaker's permission to enter? Colonel Sherman's request that she delay her visit had been tantamount to a command; so had Piers' admonition about the unsafe floors a few minutes ago.

She glanced over her shoulder again, hoping that two figures would suddenly materialize on the overgrown path at the corner of the house and solve her indecision. But the path remained stubbornly empty and the only newcomers were two long-necked waterbirds that swooped down from a cypress tree and destroyed the stillness with a shattering cacophony of sound.

The disturbance served as her final motivation. She'd hung around like a child with her nose pressed to a shop window long enough. She would explore the lower floor of Bellecourt herself and Julius could fill in the details later.

Resolutely, she marched up the steps and across the sagging boards of the porch. The brass handle of the door worked stiffly but finally yielded to pressure and the thick wooden portal moved inward.

There was a sudden flow of dank air which made Sara's nose quiver when she stepped over the threshold and stood blinking in the gloom, the door still ajar behind her.

She chewed nervously on her lower lip and waited for her blindness to pass. Somehow she hadn't realized that it would be so dark . . . so utterly deserted. As if she'd moved into a different epoch merely by crossing the sill. For a second, she toyed with going back to the steps and then the decision was made when a draft closed the door behind her with a creaking thud. Sara jumped instinctively, her heart pounding like a kettledrum in her breast.

Before further reaction could set in, she leaned against the wall, calling herself all kinds of an idiot for behaving like a youngster at a horror movie. Then she straightened her shoulders and set about trying to identify the shadowy objects in the entrance hall.

The square shape to her left must be some kind of a table, she decided, not allowing herself to acknowledge that it also looked like the coffin where the stake was hammered into Count Dracula's victims. The murky spiral to her right must be the remnants of the stairway leading to the second floor, but Piers' warning about rotting steps made her decide hastily that she wouldn't investigate that! There was no reason she couldn't go on through the hall, however, now that her eyes were getting accustomed to the gloom. Somewhere at the back of the house, there must be some unshuttered windows.

Her first careful steps away from the door proved that Piers was right on another score; the wooden flooring was gone and she found herself walking on packed earth. No wonder there was such a musty smell to the inside of the house.

It was a real shame that Bellecourt had been allowed to fall into such disrepair. Colonel Sherman was right; mansions such as this should be given an honorable death rather than gradually moldering away. Suddenly she wished that Aunt Prue had disposed of her inheritance by long-distance correspondence. This last "bedside visit" was proving entirely too painful.

Then she heard a combination of sounds that made her steps freeze again. A strange snuffling came from the archway ahead of her just before the distinct thud of slow, dragging footsteps emerged from the shadows at the back of the hallway. She waited a second longer and then she turned blindly back toward the front door, groping for the newel post on the stairs to get her bearings.

Her fingers clutched the smooth wood—then flattened, nerveless, as they hit a feathered carcass slung carelessly over the bannister. Her gasp turned into a whimper of disbelief, her hand jerking back from the still-warm body as if it were red-hot.

Only when she became aware of the sticky substance oozing down her fingers did she let out a shriek of sheer terror and flung herself at the doorway in a frantic attempt to escape.

Chapter Three

"For God's sake, Sara—stop that noise! Right now, d'ye hear!"

She was so terrified that the masculine voice only vaguely penetrated her consciousness. Opening her lips to scream again, she found herself grabbed by the shoulders and shaken so hard that her head wobbled like a pumpkin on a stick.

"Don't . . . don't do that," she whimpered as she tried to resist.

The shaking subsided partially as Piers peered down into her brimming eyes. Then his own widened as he saw the blood on her palms. "My God, you're hurt! What happened?" He pushed her down on the top porch step and made her use the brick column as a backrest.

For the first time, Sara became aware that she was outside again, that the air was fresh and sweet and there was no need to sit as if her backbone had atrophied in the last ten minutes. She made a conscious effort to relax but found her gaze returning to the entrance where the door gaped open.

Piers followed her apprehensive glance and frowned. "It's okay, Sara. I just sent Julius in there to get some water. I thought you were going to pass out on me." His dark brows drew together. "Tell me what happened," he demanded again.

"I'm not sure . . ." She started to fumble for a handkerchief and gratefully accepted the one he thrust in her hand. Her gaze went down to the white linen. "I don't want to get blood on this . . ."

Piers snorted and took the handkerchief to clean the blood from her hands himself. He inspected the palms carefully when he'd finished. "That wasn't your blood. Where in the hell did it come from?"

Before Sara could reply, a bent old man with a suggestion of grizzled hair came hurrying through the door carrying a can of water. He drew up in surprise when he saw Sara and Piers talking.

Piers straightened. "Sara . . . this is Julius. Julius . . . this is Miss Nichols, who's representing the new owner of Bellecourt. The lady I told you about."

It seemed to Sara that his last words held a subtle emphasis—almost a warning. She stared at him, trying to find an answer while her thoughts were still muddled with fear.

She finally managed a smile and struggled to her feet, "How do you do, Julius. I'm happy to meet you."

"Thank you, ma'am." Julius' head bobbed with a curious birdlike movement and his wrinkled face, which was tanned to a teak color, split in a toothless grin. "Colonel Sherman said the new owner was coming, so I've been trying to get things tidy this past week. I'm sorry that you're feeling poorly." His glance went from her to the can of water in his hand

and then, obviously deciding not to waste it, emptied it over the railing onto a laurel shrub below.

Sara watched him, unable to conceal her amazement at his appearance. He was a short, wiry man without an ounce of extra flesh on him. His cheeks had hollowed over his toothless gums, giving the taut skin a cadaver-like semblance. This was intensified by the short gray hair which revealed every bony protuberance on his skull. Yet for all his mummified look, he emitted a cheerful aura and it was clear that he felt himself to be the *seigneur* of Bellecourt. It was evident in his every gesture.

"Do you feel like going through the house, ma'am? I'll light the lantern for you"—he spoke in a curious soft voice—"but it's just the front rooms that are so dark. There are no windows in the foyer ... there was no need. We used to have a chandelier in there from Italy. Genuine Murano glass with beeswax tapers." His voice sank to a reverent murmur and then went on. "The sconces came from there, too. Most beautiful things you ever did see. 'Course they're all gone now—but they could be replaced. You-all better come in and see for yourself. I'll just fix the lantern ..."

The thought of going back in that tomblike hallway made Sara pull back.

Piers saw her reluctance and frowned again. "What's the matter, Sara? What happened to you in there?"

"Nothing." She made a helpless gesture. "Nothing really happened. To me, I mean ..." She glanced at Julius and then forgot about caution. "But there was something bloody at the bottom of the stairs ... the body was still warm!"

"My God, why didn't you say so before!" Piers snapped. "Julius—get that lantern!"

The older man's cackle of laughter stopped him in his tracks. "Lordy, Mr. Lamont—there's no need for you to get upset. Miss Nichols just ran across that ol' rooster that I'm fixin' for dinner tonight. I was on my way out back with him when I saw that pesky little pig of mine rootin' in the living room. I put down the rooster and lit out after him but he got plumb away." Julius hoisted his pants higher on his slight frame and hooked his thumb over the belt. "Something's got to be done about the fencing out back. That pig's out more'n he's in."

As he spoke, Sara felt relief roll over her. To think she'd almost fainted with fright over blood from a dead chicken and the snufflings of a runaway pig. Her lips twisted in derision. It was a good thing the porker hadn't gotten any closer or the men in white coats would be coming to get her by now.

She darted a shamefaced glance at Piers to see if he was laughing at her display. Surprisingly enough, his profile was still deadly serious as he stared at the old caretaker.

"You've been warned about those animals before, Julius." His voice held the bite of authority. "Lee Sherman told me that the police had been to see you just last week."

"Good heavens, you mean the police are getting after Julius about the fencing at Bellecourt?" Sara was aghast. "That isn't fair. Maintenance is the owner's responsibility. I'm sure that my aunt didn't realize how bad things were on the estate," she added comfortingly to the older man. "Don't worry, Julius. I'll take care of the urgent things before I leave. You order that fencing right away."

Julius' face was a study in uncertainty as he stared at her. Then his mouth creased in a grin which showed his pink gums. "That's the best news I've heard, Miss Nichols." He turned to Piers with an air of dignity. "Mighty kind, don't you think, sir?"

Piers nodded. "Mighty kind, Julius. I'm glad you realize it. So from now on—no more animal troubles, understand?"

"Well, there's no need to dwell on it." Sara brushed the wrinkles from her skirt. "Now I would like to see the house if you'll get the lantern."

"Yes, ma'am ... right away." Julius started to disappear around the corner of the porch.

"And Julius!" Piers' hail halted the old man in his tracks. "Get rid of that rooster before you come back. I'd recommend the stew pot this time."

Sara watched Julius nod vigorously and then hurry out of sight. "You needn't have been so hard on him," she said, turning back to Piers, who was lounging against the column. "Now that I know the whole story, the sight of a dead rooster wouldn't give me a fit of the vapors. It was just so dark before ..."

Piers still frowned. "It should never have happened."

Sara couldn't see why he was taking the occurrence so seriously and, for a moment, was tempted to ask him. Then she realized there was no point in starting another wrangle when they were having a peaceful interlude. Besides, she reasoned, Piers *had* been a bulwark of comfort when she'd been so frightened. Diplomatically, she decided to change the subject. "Those columns are huge, aren't they?" she murmured, going up beside him and running her hand over the curved surface from which the white paint had peeled long ago. "I wonder how they made them?"

Piers' eyebrows went up in a way that told her he was quite aware of her attempt at subterfuge but his voice didn't give anything away. "Just the way the Greeks did, only the slaves made pie-shaped bricks for the Louisiana plantations." He stepped back and squinted upward. "They've held up very well. It's too bad I can't say as much for that gallery floor. It looks as if rot's set in on those supports."

Sara nodded and sighed. "And there's so much of it to fix. They did do things on a grand scale, didn't they? Venetian chandeliers and all."

"There was plenty of money in those days ... plenty of cheap labor. Owners could afford builders like Gallier who specialized in classical architecture. Then the war came and the nightmare started. Bellecourt was luckier than most. It survived, at least."

"Uh-huh." Sara leaned back against the column and shoved her hands in her jacket pockets. "I didn't know it would be like this though or I don't think I would have come."

"It would have been worse for your aunt," Piers pointed out. "Bellecourt was real to her, part of her childhood heritage. You can go back up North and forget about the whole thing as soon as you cross the state line."

LOVE'S MAGIC SPELL

"Do you really believe it's as easy as that?" she asked in a dangerously level tone.

Piers ignored her anger. "I hope not. Bellecourt is too beautiful to be slighted. That's why it deserves a second look, despite what Colonel Sherman says." He pushed erect with a sigh. "Although I'll have to admit that his idea is the sensible one. Come on, I hear Julius in the hall. Let's see what's left in the old place . . ."

"Besides the pig, you mean," she said, attempting to lighten the atmosphere.

"Definitely. The pig doesn't count as an asset."

Unfortunately, when the pig and the rooster were removed, there was little left on the ground floor of the old plantation except a walnut staircase whose wonderful lines still bore traces of an era of grandeur. Elsewhere the rooms had only floors of tamped-down dirt and walls where paper had dampened and decayed to reveal mottled plaster beneath. The elaborate ceiling friezes looked like patchwork pieces in the reception areas and seemed past restoration. All of the fireplaces had been stripped of their accessories except for marble mantels and most of those were chipped and cracked on the edges. Overhead, brass and gold-colored chains hung starkly from the centers of the rooms, the only reminders of elaborate chandeliers which once graced the premises.

After they had passed through the main chambers and were once again in the darkened hallway, Sara looked around with a puzzled expression. "I counted two drawing rooms, a dining room, and some sort of a reception room. Where was the kitchen?"

Julius started to laugh softly.

Piers smiled as well. "There speaks the northerner," he teased. "You don't find kitchens in the old plantations. The kitchen was always a separate building out back and the food was brought into the main house. It didn't do much for keeping the soup hot, but the cabbage smells stayed outside. Remember that little stairway you saw tucked away by the back door?"

Sara nodded.

"That's where the house servants took the wood and the water up to the second flcor for the bedrooms," Piers went on. "They had lots to do in those days."

She shuddered, remembering how steep those stairs were. "Sometimes I think central heating should rank right up with the invention of the wheel."

"They didn't need a furnace at Bellecourt. You just haven't seen the beautiful marble fireplaces on the upper floor," Julius said, anxious to show a few redeeming features. "Things are in better shape up there."

"The question is—how do we get there to find out," Piers said, going over to inspect the winding stair near the front door. "Will this bear our weight?"

"Oh, I hope so." Now that the newel post was without its grisly decoration, Sara was able to appreciate the design of the staircase and its beautiful proportions. The winding walnut bannister rail gleamed with the patina of age and looked in good condition although some of the treads below obviously needed repairing.

"Nothing'll happen to us," Julius assured them, "if you watch where you put your feet. Follow me and you'll be safe as in your trundle bed."

"Well . . ." Piers sounded dubious, but after a look at Sara's eager face, he gave in with a shrug. "Let's do what the man says."

They reached the upper floor without mishap although the creaking of one or two steps kept them from lingering en route. Julius apparently didn't give the ominous noises a second thought, for he could scarcely wait until Sara reached the top of the stairway to point out two formidable wooden chests in the nearest bedroom.

"I *told* you some of the treasures were left, Miss Nichols," he said triumphantly. "You can go home and tell your aunt that two of the finest armoires in Louisiana are still here at Bellecourt." He stroked the side of one lovingly. "Pure cypress, this one is . . . and just look at the way those doors fit." He opened it to illustrate.

Sara looked puzzled as she obediently peered inside. "But there's no hanging space. How could you use that for a closet?"

Both Piers and Julius smiled, but it was the former who told her, "There isn't any hanging space in early armoires. That's one of the ways you can date them. The clothing was just folded and put on the shelves."

"I give up," she laughed. "It's easy to see I'm with experts. What other goodies can I report to Aunt Prue?"

Julius beckoned her into another bedroom which was deserted except for a carved canopy bed and matching *lit de repos* in the corner. "Folks say these are mighty fine pieces. Lots of people have wanted to take 'em off my hands."

Piers whistled softly. "I can well believe it. That bed's early Victorian and in beautiful condition." He went over with Sara to inspect it more closely. "Bet you don't know what that's for," he said, indicating an intricately turned piece of wood which comprised the only footboard.

She shook her head. "It looks like a great big rolling pin, but I just thought it was support for those magnificent posters."

"Actually it can be removed," Piers told her as he reached over to show her the slotted ends, "but you're not far off with the rolling pin idea. The plantation maids used this to flatten the feather mattress when they made the bed. People occupied the *lit de repos* for naps during the day—that way they didn't muss up the big bed."

"How about that!" Sara was enthusiastically admiring. "And they talk about newfangled ideas!" She stepped back to admire the towering bed. "Isn't it the most gorgeous thing you've ever seen! Imagine a canopy to match the bedroom curtains—it'd be worth building a home just for it."

"They had to do that in one of the old plantations," Piers told her. "The plantation owner got carried away on a furniture-buying spree up North and purchased a Gothic bedroom suite originally designed for Henry Clay. When he sent the bed home, he found that the ceiling was too low in his bedroom. Couldn't even get his purchase through the door."

"What happened?"

Piers shrugged. "He simply called an architect and had a new wing added ... with higher ceilings throughout. Nothing to it," he added solemnly and then grinned. "*If* you've a half million dollars to play with."

Sara nodded ruefully and sighed as she stroked one of the bed's posters. "Well, there's no use even thinking about this beauty. It wouldn't fit in Aunt Prue's living room ... let alone her bedroom."

"She can't raise the ceiling?" Piers wanted to know.

Sara kept a solemn face. "I think the tenants in the apartment above her might object."

He grimaced. "Quite possibly."

Julius had wandered toward the far side of the room. "Just take a look at the marble on this fireplace mantel, Miss Nichols." He stroked the satiny surface with his palm. "Came right from Italy ... and the carvings are just as good as the day it arrived."

"It's beautiful, Julius." She went over to admire it. "You've taken wonderful care of all the furnishings. I had no idea these things were still in the house."

"There's lots of folks who'd be glad to buy them." He turned and nodded toward a bureau next to the long windows which faced out onto the gallery. "A man from New Orleans had heard about that and was mighty put out when it wasn't for sale."

Sara followed Piers over to the chest-high piece which gleamed in the sunlight. "You'll have to do the honors again," she admitted. "That deep drawer must mean something."

"Plenty of extra money if your aunt ever decides to sell it," he told her. "It's an authentic bird's eye maple bonnet cupboard—that's why it has the deep top drawer. The furniture market isn't glutted with them."

Sara sighed. "It's absolutely gorgeous. I'm going back to Chicago and throw out everything in my apartment except my electric can opener."

Piers' eyes glinted with amusement. "Bellecourt has everything—except a nice cut-glass flycatcher. Isn't that right, Julius?"

The old man nodded. "There used to be two or three—but they traded them for groceries about ten years ago. The cane harvest was mighty poor that year."

"Wouldn't you know!" Sara smiled. "Well, Aunt Prue can't hit the jackpot every time—and she's awfully lucky to own all this. Have we seen most of the things?"

"All the good ones," Julius admitted. "I had a chance to rent these rooms a while back. There were some movie folks who wanted to film up here but the floors wouldn't stand the weight of their equipment."

"I should think not," Piers said, testing a board with his shoe. "One camera on this floor for five minutes and the next scene would have been shot in the basement." He grinned at Sara. "Bellecourt would have been turned into a split-level design after all these years."

"We have enough headaches without that," she admitted. "Besides, I like it the way it is."

"You should have seen it the way it was," Julius muttered, almost to himself.

Sara saw him cross to the bedroom door next to the gallery and open the creaking hinges. Wordlessly she and Piers followed him out onto the broad gallery which enclosed all sides of the house.

"Twenty-five years ago they say Bellecourt was the showplace of the whole state. Folks came in buses to see it, and the governor held a reception out in the gardens." Julius' heavy eyelids came halfway down to shutter his glance as he stared onto the overgrown lawn and flowerbeds below.

Was he seeing it the way it was, Sara wondered, or was his mind back in those better days? He'd lived alone with memories so long that the possibility was more than likely.

She cleared her throat to break the spell. "This decision to sell isn't as easy as I thought. It's going to take some time."

"Probably your aunt realized that when she sent you down here." Piers said. He looked at his watch then and said, "My God, where's the time gone? We'll have to leave or we'll miss lunch at Arcady."

"And that would never do," she teased.

"Certainly not. Bellecourt will be around for many a day but stomachs have to be treated with respect. Thanks for showing us around, Julius," he said to the old caretaker as they moved inside and watched him carefully close the gallery door before leading them to the head of the winding stair.

"It was no trouble, Mr. Lamont." Julius started down the steps and they played Follow-the-Leader behind him. "Will you be coming again with the

Colonel this afternoon?" he asked Sara over his shoulder.

"Er ... I don't think so." She had already decided that she needed more time before listening to the Colonel's sales talk. Certainly she should talk to Aunt Prue before making the final decision. Still thoughtful, she followed Julius out into the daylight on the front porch. "Don't worry, though. I'll definitely be in touch with you soon to let you know what my aunt has decided."

"You'll tell her that I've been working hard to keep the old place up?" He sounded anxious.

"I'll tell her you've done a wonderful job," she said truthfully.

Piers nudged her forward. "Come on ... time to be going. Thanks again, Julius." Then, almost as an afterthought, he paused on the porch steps to look back and say, "You *will* be careful with those animals of yours, won't you? I'd hate to see you get into any more trouble."

"There's no need for folks to worry. I'll see that they don't bother nobody." There was a truculence in the old man's tone. "The law says that if they stay on Bellecourt land———"

"That's all anybody's asking," Piers cut in tersely. "We'll see you later."

Sara waited until they were almost to the main gate before she murmured. "What's all the big fuss about animals? Julius doesn't have anything very big to crawl through the fence, does he?"

"Not much. At least, not now." Piers motioned her through the iron barrier and then helped her into the car. "A couple years ago, he had a few head of cattle. Now I guess he's down to a pig and some chickens." As he turned to check for oncoming traffic before pulling out on the road, he surprised a wistful expression on her face. She was staring silently back at the outline of the big house still visible at the end of the drive. Piers smiled slightly to himself and drove off without commenting.

The journey to Arcady took only a few minutes longer and a comfortable silence existed between them on the way. Sara was busy with her thoughts, although it was impossible to ignore Piers' relaxed figure beside her. She wondered why she had ever thought that he was hard to get along with. Certainly she couldn't fault his manners during their time at Bellecourt. That knowledge made her voice warmer than usual as she finally turned to him and said, "It was nice of you to take all this time. I hope it hasn't inconvenienced you."

"Not at all." His tone was pleasantly impersonal. "I thought you should see the old place before the Colonel started his 'hard sell.'"

"I *have* met salesmen before and managed to muddle through."

"Yes, but they don't all come equipped with sons like Lee. Stephanie tells me that he's dynamite. Remember that and act accordingly if you have dinner with him tomorrow night."

"Don't be ridiculous! Colonel Sherman wouldn't try anything like that. Your friend Stephanie must have been exaggerating." She raised her chin defiantly as she stared at his profile.

"Ummm." Plainly he wasn't convinced. "We'll see.

It doesn't hurt to keep your eyes open anyway. Lee's pretty devastating when it comes to women."

"Are you trying to tell me that I can't cope with someone like Lee Sherman at my age?" she asked with dangerous calm.

"My dear girl, I'm not suggesting anything of the sort."

"I'm *not* your dear girl!" She stirred on the seat, determined to put all the distance possible between them. "Honestly, you are the most irritating person! I should have known that you had something unpleasant on your mind when you came along in the first place. Why don't you just admit that you wanted to get in your licks first . . . before Lee and the Colonel had a chance."

His jaw firmed stubbornly. "Because I knew that you'd erupt like Krakatoa if I did. Why in the devil do you have to be so stubborn when you're given some good advice. I *told* Stephanie that you'd never listen—" He broke off at her angry exclamation, belatedly aware that he'd dropped a clanger.

"Well, you were right about *that*, at least," she told him after the awkward silence. "And you might impress Stephanie once and for all that I don't need any more advice from either of you. What's more, you can tell her . . ."

"Dammit! You can tell her yourself," he snapped as they turned into a gravel cul-de-sac. "This is Arcady."

Sara dragged her glance from his angry profile to stare at a cluster of buildings surrounding a parklike square. Along one side, there was a large restaurant building with a porch in front where patrons sat on

LOVE'S MAGIC SPELL

bentwood rocking chairs while they waited for their table reservations. Other visitors were thronging into an extensive gift shop at the back of the square. Over at the right she noticed a two-story guest house for overnight accommodation. Huge shade trees were everywhere, giving the busy inn a placid atmosphere despite its obvious popularity.

Sara blinked in confusion. "Is this where I stay?"

"None other." Piers turned off the ignition with an angry movement. "Don't blame me if you don't like it. The Colonel arranged this on his own."

"Then what did you mean about telling Stephanie?" she persisted, determined to continue the quarrel.

"Just what I said. I told you she'd be around," he opened the door and got out, jerking his head toward a blond figure in a familiar blue denim skirt floating down the path toward them.

"You knew all along, didn't you?" It was a dull statement rather than a question but she had the answer before Piers could even open his mouth to reply.

Stephanie pulled up beside him and stood on tiptoe to kiss his cheek. "Sweetie—I thought you were nevah comin'," she drawled. "This is the second day in a row you've kept me waitin' for a lunch date." Then she turned to Sara and bestowed her unruffled smile. "How do you like the looks of Arcady, Sara? Be sure and let me know if there's anything I can do."

Sara got out of the car and carefully avoided Piers' mocking expression. "You've done too much already," she said carefully.

"That's right, Steff," his voice was still edged

with anger. "Sara was just saying that she wanted to thank you in person."

Stephanie threw out her hands and beamed at both of them. "Well, let's discuss it over lunch. You can see your room later, Sara."

"Oh, no . . . really. It isn't necessary."

"Stop being kittenish and come along," Piers gestured toward the restaurant.

Sara rounded on him. "I'm *not* being kittenish!"

"What other reason could you possibly have for skipping lunch?" he asked, still sounding annoyed. "Stephanie will think you're looking for an excuse to avoid us."

Sara's glance hovered at his shoe tops. "That isn't true. I don't want to intrude."

"What nonsense! Let's go eat." Stephanie urged her along the path. "Frankly, I'm starving and the chef has saved some Chicken Jambalaya for us."

Piers fell in step beside Stephanie but he managed to give Sara a mocking look as he said, "Arcady's a showplace of real southern hospitality. Now you'll have plenty to talk about when you go home again."

"Oh, I know." Her sarcasm matched his. "And I've learned so much from all of you that I'm up to here already." She measured her throat with the edge of her palm. "Much more and I'm going to . . . choke," she deliberately hesitated over the last word.

Piers' gray eyes ran over her coldly. "Let me know if there's any way I can help," was all he said.

Chapter Four

Lunch wasn't quite the ordeal that Sara anticipated.

Stephanie either chose to overlook the coolness between her two guests or wasn't even aware of its existence. She was so interested in hearing Sara's reaction to Bellecourt that anything else was completely ignored. "I knew you'd be impressed!" she said once they were seated at a round table in the corner of the sunny dining room and their order had been taken. "Bellecourt is the most gorgeous old place in the state. I've been drooling over it for years. You'd never know that I'm a charter member of the Historical Society, would you?"

Piers leaned back in his chair and surveyed her fondly. "I *did* mention the fact." His warm expression changed appreciably as he glanced at Sara. "But you'd better take Stephanie's and my opinions with a considerable dose of salt—they're definitely prejudiced."

"Why? There's nothing wrong with feeling strongly about a subject," Stephanie told him. "If there's anything that bores me it's those people whose pants are shiny from straddling every issue that comes along. Frankly I prefer a nice refreshing bigot with opinions every time—they make life much more interesting."

Piers turned to Sara again. "That's why Stephanie's so fond of my company. I haven't seen both sides of an issue in years, which makes me fit right in."

It was disconcerting, Sara thought, to find him so adept at reading her mind.

Stephanie merely gave him that slow warm smile of hers, which indicated that she liked him precisely the way he was. Then she leaned forward to pass the butter to Sara. "I forgot to ask whether you'd met Julius on your tour."

"Oh, yes—he was there."

"Very much so," Piers said. "He almost scared Sara out of her skin right at the beginning." Stephanie's sudden silence made him add quickly, "It was nothing serious. He'd just parked one of his roosters in an inconvenient spot and she happened on to it."

Sara felt she should explain, "I wouldn't have minded, except that he'd just cut its throat." Her voice faltered. "It was silly of me to be frightened ... but I didn't know what it was at first."

"Oh, dear—what a shame." Stephanie's voice was soft with understanding. "I hope you weren't too upset. Julius is careless about some things, but he's an old man and we've all made allowances over the years."

"That's all very well—as far as it goes," Piers sounded stubborn. "But these days Julius uses advanced age as an excuse for everything from his aching corns to stealing from the Sherman's vegetable garden."

"Lee didn't mind Julius' midnight raids," Stephanie replied. "He just suggested that Julius take some of the carrots as well as the tomatoes and melons."

"That's beside the point. It's time somebody called a halt to Julius' escapades. Now the Bellecourt has changed owners, the problem may solve itself."

"Piers! That isn't fair," Stephanie cut in without giving Sara a chance to reply. "You don't pull down an estate like Bellecourt just so Julius will stop making a nuisance of himself."

Sara put down her butter knife with an air of finality. "Look, if you're hoping to influence me over lunch or something, then I might as well make one thing clear right now. My aunt simply can't afford to keep the place ... no matter how much she'd like to." She started to push back her chair. "If you'll excuse me—I'll let you enjoy your meal in peace and quiet."

Piers reached over to capture her wrist with a grip of iron, pulling her back down again. "*Will* you sit down and behave yourself."

Stephanie's laughter bubbled out as she leaned back in her chair and surveyed them both. "He's right, you know," she confided to Sara. "If the chef heard about you walking out without giving his Jambalaya a chance, he'd be after all of us with a cleaver." Then, turning her attention to Piers, she added mildly. "And if you don't let go of her, she won't be able to sample our Arcady bread with the gumbo. It's really something special," she added to Sara as she passed a plate of napkin-wrapped hot bread. "It adds inches to your waistline, of course, but who cares?"

Sara found herself meekly relaxing in her chair as a cheerful waiter placed an appetizing bowl of gumbo in front of her. She darted a quick glance toward Piers, but he was calmly picking up his soup spoon and starting to eat as if nothing had happened.

Then the pungent fragrance of gumbo seasoning reached Sara's nostrils and she abandoned any more thoughts of escape. She broke off a piece of Arcady bread and buttered it, her reluctance vanishing as she realized how delicious it was and how hungry the morning's activities had made her. "I see why you have such a big dining room here," she told Stephanie after the first spoonful of soup.

The older woman looked pleased. "People come here from all over the South to try our specialties. Tonight the chef's featuring soft-shell crabs ... it's a pity that you won't be here to try them."

Sara's soup spoon stopped midway to her mouth and Piers' figure tensed in his chair.

"What's happening tonight? Why won't she be here to try them?" he asked Stephanie quietly.

"Because of Lee's message, of course." She grimaced abruptly then and her hand flew up to her mouth. "Oh, for heaven's sake—I forgot that you hadn't registered and collected your messages," she told Sara. "How dim can I get?"

Her southern drawl was as vexed as Sara had ever heard it. "You mean that Lee phoned?" she asked, confused.

Stephanie's fair head nodded vigorously. "About fifteen minutes ago—I took the call myself. He was pretty irritated that you hadn't checked in yet." She turned to Piers. "He's going to have words with you later about that." When he didn't deign to answer, her gaze settled back on Sara. "Anyhow, Lee said that his plans had changed and he wanted to have dinner with you tonight instead of tomorrow— if that's all right."

"I see," Sara murmured. "Can I call him back?"

" 'Fraid not. He mentioned that he'd be out all afternoon but that he'll pick you up about five thirty." Stephanie smiled. "He also asked me to tell you to take a warm wrap because he planned to paint New Orleans red and it would take a while."

Sara felt a tremor of excitement go through her. She shot a quick glance at Piers' stony profile and let her lips curve in satisfaction. "I think it sounds marvelous," she told Stephanie. "There are lots of things I'm dying to see in New Orleans."

"Well, now's your chance. Lee has had plenty of experience." There was no malice in Stephanie's tone; she was merely stating a fact. "Make him take you to a jazz concert sometime after dinner. Men usually just think about eating; they forget that women need soul food as well as stoking with calories." She shot a mischievous look at Piers. "I'm not sure you're old enough to hear this."

He calmly went on buttering some bread. "Go ahead with your gems of wisdom. I need all the help I can get."

Stephanie chuckled and reached over to pat his hand. "Such false modesty, sweetie. You wrote the book."

Sara almost choked. It was fortunate for her sense of dignity that the waiter appeared just then with a steaming platter of Chicken Jambalaya which he placed in the center of the table.

Why did it have to be chicken, she wondered ruefully and then shook her head irritably. A psychiatrist could have a field day with her if she kept on at this rate. Chicken Jambalaya at Arcady was quite different from Julius' candidate for the stew pot. Anything else was mere fancy on her part.

Strangely enough, Piers seemed relieved for the sudden silence which fell over the table. They helped themselves to the tender fowl and steaming mounds of rice while another waiter deposited dishes of okra in tomato sauce alongside. The spicy smell coming from the food made Sara smile. It was a good thing they served plenty of water at each meal, she decided. Creole seasoning had a delayed reaction, but the red pepper sauce eventually made itself felt either by taking off the roof of her mouth or calmly eating away her stomach lining. She picked up her fork and took a cautious bite. Then a more enthusiastic one. After all, stomach linings could learn to cope, and this was definitely too good to miss.

When they finally left the luncheon table, Sara felt like curling up in a chair on the wide veranda as the Inn's tortoise-shell cat was doing. Instead, she made herself tend to the formalities of registering before following Stephanie to a room in the guest wing. Piers had taken himself off with the evasive comment that he'd be "around" when Stephanie tried to pin him down. To Sara, he offered no comment at all except for a casual nod when she thanked him for transporting her to Arcady.

"Honestly, that man!" Stephanie said in an exasperated outburst as she led the way down a shaded path toward a porch at the end of the two-story building. "Trying to get Piers to commit himself is next to impossible." She shrugged then. "I suppose I should know better after all these years. Even his sister doesn't have any luck at it. I went to school with her. She swears that she never knows what Piers is going to do from one minute to another."

Sara found herself more curious than she would have liked. "He told me he was between jobs and trying to decide what to choose next."

"Oh heavens, I don't mean work." Stephanie brushed aside the problem of making a living as if it didn't count. "There's no trouble about that. Piers is one of the best sugar men in the country, so he can pick and choose. I'm talking about his private life. He goes from one woman to another like a bee gathering pollen . . . enjoying all the flowers on the way," she added darkly. She pulled up before unlocking the door to Sara's room. "That's why he gets so censorious about Lee's conquests—it takes one to know one." She motioned Sara in and changed to a hotel hostess with the next breath. "Your bags should be here by now. Ah, there they are in the corner." She flicked a switch next to the window. "This controls the air-conditioning. It's better to keep the windows closed. There *are* mosquitoes around," she admitted, "although we don't mention them in the Inn's brochures."

Sara nodded and surveyed the sitting room thoughtfully. It was sparsely but adequately furnished with two chintz-covered settees, a low table, and a small television set on a bookcase along one wall. Bright scatter rugs covered pine floors. She moved over to peer into an adjoining bedroom where a monstrous double bed with a crocheted white spread occupied most of the space.

"Your bath's just beyond," Stephanie waved toward a dressing cubicle by the bedroom area. "This doesn't match the Lafayette in comfort but frankly"—she smiled disarmingly—"the food's better. That's the kind of interior decoration our guests want."

"This looks just fine, thanks," Sara said truthfully. "I'd better get unpacked if I'm going out to dinner tonight."

Stephanie nodded and watched her shift a suitcase onto a nearby luggage rack and open it. She waited until two dresses and a pantsuit had been transferred to some hangers before she said carefully, "Sara . . ."

The other turned reluctantly, as if sensing what was coming next.

Stephanie ignored the unencouraging response, "I'm as bad as Piers about giving advice, but I hope you'll watch your step with Lee tonight. He's pretty heady stuff if he makes up his mind to turn on the charm."

Sara was carefully polite. "I'm just going out for dinner, so you needn't worry. I managed to survive dinner last night with your friend Piers."

Stephanie winced visibly. "I had a sneaking suspicion I shouldn't have said anything. Forget it, please."

"I know you meant it for the best."

"But you'd prefer that I minded my own business.

The point's taken—loud and clear. Let me know if you need anything. When I'm not being an interfering woman, I run a fairly good hotel." She pushed her hair carelessly from her face. "Incidentally, breakfast's served until ten tomorrow morning. No room service but the drop biscuits are pretty special—so don't miss it. See you later, honey."

She had closed the door behind her before Sara could reply.

Sara hung a skirt on a wire hanger and then walked over to stare through the small-paned window. Why, she wondered, was she being warned on all sides? It was like a row of dominoes toppling; each piece which fell brought a chain reaction from the others. Stephanie against Lee, Lee against Piers, and Piers against Julius ... the Colonel ... Lee ... and Sara Nichols from Chicago. She smiled as she thought about it. Piers was a regular Mrs. Grundy with all his rules and regulations.

Yet there was something unreal about the whole thing; as if all of them were paying lip service to convention but not mentioning the real object of their worries. Which was Bellecourt, of course.

Sara pressed her forehead against the cool glass of the window. If they all hadn't worked so hard being casual, it probably would never have occurred to her.

The phone rang shortly after that. Colonel Sherman had heard that she'd already toured the plantation and wondered if he could postpone their date under the circumstances? That business matter he'd hoped to close was still pending so if she didn't mind ...

Sara didn't and told him so, scarcely able to hide

her relief. The appointment was rescheduled for the next morning. Just before he hung up, the Colonel told her to have an enjoyable evening in New Orleans. "Make Lee take you along to Jackson Square and then show you the Cathedral in the moonlight. No visitor should miss it—especially a young lady."

"I'll make a note of it." She was thinking that the Arcady grapevine was working at top speed despite Louisiana siesta time. "You'll call tomorrow morning, Colonel?"

"Without fail. There is no reason why we can't get things well under way. I have the papers ready for a signature."

"We'll discuss it then," she promised before ringing off. For a second she stood staring at the receiver she'd just replaced, wondering why she'd been chary about admitting that she had Aunt Prue's power of attorney, so that her signature would be all that was necessary. Then she sighed and went over to sit down on the side of the bed and slip off her shoes. There was plenty of time later to volunteer the information.

Lee was every bit the southern gentleman when he came to collect her later that afternoon. He phoned from the office to say he was waiting on the veranda if she was ready.

Sara felt a little shy of running the gamut of tourist glances as she crossed the square, but the frank admiration in Lee's eyes as he came down the steps to greet her put all other thoughts from her mind.

"Sara, honey—you look dazzling." His pleased

glance passed over her from head to toe and didn't miss a thing on the way.

Sara was glad that she'd taken extra time over her appearance and that she'd brought along her favorite dress in tangerine chiffon which had devastated her clothes budget when she'd bought it. Draped over her shoulders was another extravagance; an Italian knit evening stole of exquisite design.

Since Lee was wearing a dark silk suit and white shirt which did magnificent things for his tanned skin, she was happy that she'd dressed for the occasion.

He confirmed her feelings as he tucked her into a white sports car. "I've made reservations for dinner at Antoine's as a starter ... then we can catch the shows on Bourbon Street later. I wasn't sure just how much of a jazz fan you were."

"I'm game for most anything." She made a grab for the door handle as he accelerated. "It shouldn't take us long to get back to New Orleans at this rate," she added wryly.

"No, not long," he confirmed and then grinned. "Sorry about that." The car's speed dropped perceptibly. "I forgot that you weren't used to my driving."

"It *is* a little different from your father's."

"My God, I should hope so," he snorted. "Otherwise we'd be packing a lunch to eat on the way."

"That's pure exaggeration. I get the feeling this is an old score."

"One of many." Lee's tone was blithe. "When two generations live together—the way Dad and I do—something's got to give." He shot a sidelong glance her way. "Actually, his blood pressure suffers more than mine. It's a good thing I'm the only fledgling in the nest or I would have been bumped out into the cold world long ago. We've tangled over more than speed laws, believe me."

Sara wasn't sure she wanted to be plunged into an intimate glimpse of the Shermans' private lives. "Family affairs can get a little complicated at times," she said, trying to pass it off lightly.

"That's an understatement," Lee slowed for an arterial and then zoomed onto it without an appreciable slackening of speed. "This is a shortcut to the freeway," he explained. "It cuts a good half hour off our time."

She felt like asking him why they were in such a tremendous hurry but decided against it. Instead she compromised by saying, "I gather that you get into the city often?"

"Every chance I get. Much too often for my father's peace of mind." He fumbled in his shirt pocket for his cigarettes and brought the package out to offer it to Sara.

She shook her head and waited until he'd lit his with the dashboard lighter. "What's so bad about driving into New Orleans?"

"That's what I'd like to know." His voice was truculent. "Dad's of the old school. You know the type; eight hours sleep and up at dawn in case something's happened to the damn cane crop overnight."

"And does it ever?"

"What?"

"Happen to the cane crop overnight?"

His broad shoulders shrugged. "Search me. I've never been up when the dew's on to see. 'Early ripe—early rotten' is my motto."

"The simile's a little blurred but I get the idea. If you don't like cane farming and living in the country, why do you do it?"

Lee groaned but kept his attention straight ahead as he passed a slow-moving tanker truck. "That should be evident at first glance." When she didn't reply, he half-turned to say, "Money, my love. It's as simple as that."

"There must be other ways to make a living."

"Well, I'm a little old to go back to school." He moved restlessly. "Besides, things aren't always as bad as I let on, so don't take me too seriously. It's just that I'm tired of finding little memos on the breakfast table that say 'Try Harder.' "

Her lips quivered with laughter as she surveyed his well-turned-out appearance and the sleek lines of the expensive car. "But you're not poised on the railing of the bridge?"

"Hardly." He chuckled in response. "Nor down to selling our last flycatcher."

"Just my luck!" She pulled her stole more comfortably around her shoulders and settled back against the leather seat. "When that day comes, send me a telegram. That's the only way I'll ever get one of the lovely things."

"Oh, I don't know—there might be others." He twirled an imaginary waxed moustache. "How much is it worth to you, my fair beauty?"

She laughed delightedly. "Ask me again after dinner. Maybe I'll have mellowed by then."

He pretended to make a note. "After dinner it is. Speaking of questions—what in the dickens took you so long to get to Arcady today? Piers must have detoured through Mississippi or Arkansas. He always *did* take advantage of everything that came his way."

"Not this time," she said. "He just drove me to Bellecourt so I could satisfy my curiosity. I thought that your father had told you." She frowned slightly as she stared at his profile. "He knew about it when he called this afternoon."

"Then he heard about it from somebody else. Dad doesn't fit social amenities into our business calls." Annoyance was back in his voice again. "If you looked over Bellecourt, you must have met Julius. How did you like him?"

"Just fine," Sara replied, wondering if liking Julius was some sort of a hidden password. "He seems to be devoted to the estate."

"Absolutely loyal," Lee confirmed. "One of the old school and believe me, they're a vanishing race."

"Would your father keep him on if Aunt Prue accepts his offer for the property?"

"That depends. If Bellecourt is turned into more cane acreage, I don't suppose we'd need a real caretaker." Lee rubbed his jaw thoughtfully. "But I can't see anybody dislodging Julius if he makes up his mind to stay. There'll always be a place for him."

Sara sighed. "Well, that's something. Old family retainers aren't a problem in Chicago."

"It isn't on the priority list here, either," Lee assured her. "Now, let's think of more pleasant things, like what we're going to eat tonight and what we'll do after that."

"Your father suggested Jackson Square and the Cathedral . . ."

"He would." Lee's frown faded as he thought it over. "On the other hand, maybe the old man's right. We'll need a cup of coffee at the French Market to stay awake on the drive home—so let's take it as it comes."

Sara found that "it" came very well.

Dinner at Antoine's lived up to all she'd heard about the famed restaurant. When ordering, she reluctantly turned down their popular *Pompano en Papillote* for Beef Tenderloin with Sauce Béarnaise, accompanied by a potato soufflé and green salad. Lee happily consumed the inevitable bowl of Chicken Filé Gumbo and a monstrous plateful of Oysters Rockefeller.

Afterward they joined the throngs of sightseers along Bourbon and Royal streets on a warm evening that felt more like June than November.

Music and merriment were the main order of business in New Orleans night life with uninhibited floor shows and uninhibited pedestrians who were anxious to see it all. Shop windows on the tourist beat were a jumble of praline boxes, voodoo dolls, and marvelously aromatic chickory coffee. Grocery stores hawked gumbo recipes next to towering displays of filé seasoning and the inevitable bottles of Tabasco sauce which were placed alongside the sugar bowl on most New Orleans restaurant tables.

Tucked in between the food displays were the wonderful antique shops. Their prices would have had New Orleans' pioneers turning restlessly in their famed family tombs which were displayed above ground level at the city's outskirts.

As Sara and Lee circled back into Bourbon Street, they made their way to a crowded nightclub. The room was dimly lit and the air hung blue with smoke as spotlights focused on a tiny raised stage where some musicians were assembling. The management didn't even make a token gesture toward a cocktail pianist or routine burlesque acts. Jazz was the order of the night in that crowded room—the only reason for its existence.

Then Sara and the rest of the audience forgot such trivialities as the concert began.

For two hours the clarinets and the saxophones moaned—the stringed bass was low-down and soul-searching and a bank of trumpets blared their defiance. In the middle of the stage a long-haired drummer methodically went wild at specified intervals.

When the concert was over and the audience filed out onto the street, Sara's head was spinning but her mind felt as if it had been shaken and then hung out in a stiff breeze to dry. Every cobweb was gone and sometime during the evening she had recovered her zest for simply being alive.

"It was marvelous," she told Lee, "but half the magic was hearing it in New Orleans. Jazz isn't the same up North or on television or"—her hands fluttered out—"anywhere." She gestured at the people crowded around them on the narrow street decorated with the wrought-iron grills of the Vieux Carré. "I hadn't realized before but every night is like Mardi Gras here, isn't it?"

LOVE'S MAGIC SPELL

"One long holiday—on the surface, at least," Lee agreed. "I can't imagine living anywhere else. And I don't intend to—for very long. But that's enough of serious talk." He caught her arm firmly against his side. "You must be hungry again by now."

"You have to be fooling," she said, pulling to a stop and then hastily moving on again as two sailors collided with her in the good-natured throng.

"Watch it," Lee laughed. "Never stop at an intersection without signaling. You'll get run over in the crush."

"I can believe it." She stayed close by his tall figure. "All right, *you* tell me—where are we heading?"

"We'll take Dad's advice and strike out for the French Market. It'll be less crowded than here and I can use some coffee before the drive home. Okay?"

"Of course." She lengthened her steps, trying to keep up with his long strides as they turned into a side street and made their way toward the river.

Jackson Square was full of strolling couples but there was none of Bourbon Street's raucous accompaniment. The lofty architecture of the Cathedral provided ecclesiastical dignity for the surroundings, and the lush greenery of the mini-park added beauty of a more earthly variety.

The French Market blazed with light as they found a place at an outdoor table and were promptly served with chickory coffee mixed with hot milk in the French style and two platefuls of special doughnuts.

Lee chuckled as he watched Sara investigate hers.

"They're called *beignets*," he explained, "but they taste like regular doughnuts."

"Except that they look like little square pillows covered with powdered sugar." She picked one up and took a bite. "Umm ... delicious! They're still warm from the oven."

Lee reached for his plate. "Naturally. I don't suppose there's a vitamin in a carload, but the menu hasn't changed in years." He chewed reflectively before swallowing some coffee. "It seems a shame to end the evening but I suppose we'd better be on our way. Otherwise, I'll never make it to that damned mill in the morning. You wouldn't like to come down and visit me, would you?" he asked hopefully. "I do a first-rate personally conducted tour. No charge for beautiful brunettes."

Her lips quirked. "It's the best offer I've had tonight. Besides, I would like to see a sugar mill; I don't imagine I'll be down this way again once Bellecourt is sold. I'd better check with your father first though, before I make any plans for tomorrow."

"Don't worry about that." Lee's tone was careless. "I'll clear it with the old man at breakfast. There's no reason I can't take you through the mill and then drop you at Bellecourt so you can talk business with him."

"Well, if you're sure ..."

He grinned confidently. "Just leave it to me, honey. Now drink your coffee. Both of us might as well have insomnia on the drive home. I expect my dates to provide scintillating chatter all the way."

Sara wouldn't have used that adjective to describe their sporadic bursts of conversation en route, but the miles disappeared effortlessly on the drive back to Arcady. The freeway going north was virtually deserted other than an occasional truck and Lee kept his speedometer at the legal limit all the way, only easing up on the accelerator when he turned into the gravel drive at the Inn.

Sara noted that there wasn't a soul in sight, which wasn't surprising considering the early morning hour. Two spotlights bathed the inner square of the Inn with soft illumination and the only other light came from hooded installations at the edge of the paths leading to the guest wings.

Lee cut his engine and let the car roll to a stop at the side of the parking area. Then he sighed and turned on the seat, resting his arm over her shoulders. "I'm sorry to say that this concludes the New Orleans by Night tour. However, madame, if you'd care to leave any gratuities for the driver, they'll be gratefully accepted."

Sara smiled as she reached for the door handle. "I understood when I bought my ticket that all gratuities were included. You mean there's an additional charge?"

Lee's thick eyebrows went up in reproof. "We prefer to consider it in the nature of a donation."

"I see." Sara kept her tone as solemn as his. "Just what did you have in mind?"

"Well, normally I don't include goodnight kisses on a first tour. Of course, that rule was drawn up for my local patrons..."

She nodded. "It isn't quite the same for out-of-towners, is it?"

"Exactly. You can't count on repeat business."

His arm curved more tightly about her shoulders.

She put up a firm hand to keep it there. "Don't forget—there's the sugar mill tour tomorrow if everything goes as scheduled."

"Ummm." He brushed off her restraining fingers and pulled her toward him. "I'll collect in advance—if you don't mind. It's the only way to do business."

His lips came down to cover hers with a proficiency that could only have come from long practice. However, that didn't detract one whit from the pleasure of it. It was only when he raised his head to pull her into a more comfortable position that Sara put a firm hand against his chest. It was obvious Lee wasn't accustomed to having his lovemaking abruptly terminated.

"One tour—one kiss," she told him, gathering her stole and opening the car door. Then she smiled. "Thank you for a lovely evening. I had a wonderful time."

He opened his door and started to get out. "At least, let me see you to your room . . ."

Sara shook her head, having no desire to drag out the leave-taking. "That isn't necessary. I'll see you tomorrow, then—thanks again." She blew him a kiss before turning and hurrying along the path toward the guest wing. For a moment or two, there was no sound except her heels tapping along the brick walk. Then came the slam of the car door and the roar of the engine as Lee gunned it to life. From the way he drove out onto the highway, Sara gathered that he was more annoyed by her abrupt leave-taking than she'd imagined. Her steps slowed and she frowned as she thought about it. At least they hadn't exchanged

LOVE'S MAGIC SPELL

any harsh words so there would be no apologies due when they met the next morning.

She was so intent on burrowing in her purse for her room key that she didn't see a tall masculine figure materialize from a side path until he fell into step behind her.

"A little late, aren't you?" came a familiar male voice.

"Oh, good lord!" She gave such a start that she wobbled and almost lost her footing on the uneven bricks. "Must you creep up and scare people half to death," she complained to Piers. "You nearly gave me a heart attack!"

"Strange, I thought you were having *that* in the car earlier. It was a very touching performance."

"I didn't know we had an audience." She scowled at him. "Can't you find better things to do?"

"My God!" His voice changed from sarcasm to anger. "*I* should be the one who's complaining. There I was, crouched behind a damned tree trunk just so I wouldn't embarrass you. If you had dragged things out much longer, I could've gotten pneumonia."

"Well, if you suffer any ill effects, just send your doctor's bill to me," she countered in the same tone. "Now, if you'll excuse me . . ." She started off again and took a half dozen steps before she turned angrily to add, "You *don't* have to see me to the door. I'm perfectly able to take care of myself."

Piers paused beside her and shoved his hands in his pockets as he stared down at her stormy features. "That soppy leave-taking with Lee didn't do much for your disposition," he observed. "But just for the record, I have a room in the same wing and the last I heard, this path was still a public thoroughfare."

Sara flushed, furious that he had the last word every time they tangled. "Since when has a simple goodnight kiss come under the category of a 'soppy leave-taking'? If *you* tried acting like a gentleman occasionally, you might have better luck with those 'willing victims' of yours!" She pulled her stole around her shoulders with a regal gesture and prepared to sweep past him. "You might ask Lee for some pointers..."

It was, she thought, a splendid exit line.

Or would have been, if Piers hadn't caught her elbow as she brushed past and yanked her roughly against him.

"You have one hell of a nerve!" he grated out. "The way you give advice, it's no wonder your family sent you down here. They probably broke out the champagne after they got you out of town."

Sara was so incensed by the unfair accusation that for a second she forgot to struggle in his iron grasp. "You're out of your mind—I had to beg my father to come. Now will you let me go!" She tried to bang ineffectually against his chest with her free hand which was already clutching her evening bag. Naturally the effort had all the effects of a housefly storming the side of an armadillo.

Piers loftily ignored her struggles. Indeed he used his other hand to pluck her purse away from his chest like a troublesome crumb. "Well, I doubt if you had to cancel many social engagements when you left. Or don't you bother advising the men in your home town?"

"It isn't necessary." Sara stopped squirming and decided to brazen it out. She stared up at him coolly. "You're the first man I've had to Indian-wrestle since I was eight years old. Now—if you don't mind—I'd like to go in and go to bed. It's late."

"So it is, but this won't take long." Piers might have been commenting on the weather. "Let's get back to those pointers that Lee could give me."

"There's no need to go over that," she said hastily.

"Oh, but there is. I don't mind a substitute instructor." He yanked her tight against him, adding sardonically as he bent his head, "Tell me if I do anything wrong."

Then his lips parted hers, scorching them in a kiss so devastating that Sara's defenses collapsed at the outset. There wasn't an ounce of sweet affection in it; instead it was implacably demanding and so expertly sensual that her reason collapsed along with her resistance. As the embrace lengthened, she moved even closer and her hands found their way upward of their own accord to softly caress his shoulders and the back of his head.

It was Piers who finally pulled away. He took a deep breath and had to steady her tremulous figure as he released her. Silently, he reached down for her stole and purse which had fallen to the ground.

Sara stared at them as if she had never seen them before. Then one hand flew up to her mouth as she drew a quick, ragged breath.

"Sara . . . don't look like that." Piers had trouble getting the words out. "I'm sorry . . ."

"Oh, please—just get out of my way!" Clutching

her belongings as if they were a lifeline, she turned and blindly stumbled down the path toward her room.

Piers stared after her. "Damn!" he muttered. The word was low and heartfelt. His shoulders sagged and he rubbed the back of his neck wearily, aware that he'd let his anger carry him into an untenable and unforgivable position. If Sara had disliked him before, there would be no quarter given now. He thrust his hands deeply into his pockets and kicked at a stone on the path as he moved on toward the guest wing.

He was so intent on his thoughts that he almost missed the figure slumped against the porch railing as he approached. Then he heard Sara's shuddering sob and forgot what had happened as he covered the steps in a single bound. One look at her glazed expression and parchment-like complexion made him grasp her shoulders. "Sara . . . what is it? What's the matter? For God's sake—tell me."

She didn't answer. She couldn't. Physically it was all she could do to raise a trembling finger and point to the door of her room.

Scowling, Piers turned to look.

There, hanging from the doorknob on a stained, dirty string, was the battered remnant of a common garden mole. Drops of blood dripped onto the floor from the carcass . . . a carcass from which the paws had been removed—leaving only severed stumps as a grisly reminder.

Chapter Five

It didn't take long for the reaction to set in. Although the next few minutes were mainly a muddled blur to Sara, she was faintly aware of Piers finding her key, hustling her into her sitting room and depositing her on a davenport. Stephanie appeared shortly after that, dressed in slacks and a sweater that looked as if they were the first things she'd found on her closet door.

When Piers disappeared, the noises from the porch proved to Sara that he'd taken the grisly decoration with him.

Stephanie made no attempt to hide her irritation. "Honestly, I'm terribly sorry that this happened," she said, trailing Sara into the bedroom and perching on the edge of the bed as she watched her start to undress. "God knows who could have dreamed up a horror like that. We've never had that kind of problem at Arcady before."

Sara took off her sandals and replaced them in her suitcase. "What do you mean—at Arcady? You make it sound as if dissecting helpless creatures is a common practice around here."

Stephanie's glance dropped before her incredulous

one. "Not exactly ... but don't forget that Louisiana is close to the Caribbean. Some of the religious cults in this area have different ideas from up North."

Sara leaned against the wall as if she couldn't believe what she'd heard. Already her emotions felt as if they'd endured a runaway ride on a roller coaster and barely survived. That devastating embrace with Piers had shaken her more than she cared to remember even before finding the grim sacrifice decorating her door. She moved her head wearily. "What maniac could attach any religious significance to killing a poor little mole? The thing's positively barbaric!"

"Lots of superstitions are." Stephanie got up in some relief when a knock sounded on the hall door. "That'll be your hot milk. If you drink some after you take a tranquilizer, you should be able to get a decent night's sleep. Or at least manage to sleep through what's left of it."

She disappeared into the outer room and was back with an insulated chrome carafe by the time Sara had put on her pajamas and was shrugging into a short robe.

"Here you are." Stephanie poured a glass and reached into her pocket to pull out a small bottle of pills.

Sara shook her head. "I'll take the milk, thanks—but I don't need anything else. I'll be fine, honestly," she insisted at Stephanie's worried look.

"Well, if you're sure." She put the carafe on the bed table. "There's more in here if you'd like it. Piers will be furious if I don't have you follow his instructions—" She broke off lamely at Sara's sudden frown. "If there's nothing else I can do, I'll go and let you get some sleep. And don't worry about that ... thing ... on the door. Piers took care of it."

Sara nodded. The other woman was almost to the door before she said, "Stephanie—just a second. You were going to tell me about that superstition before the milk came."

"There's no need to go into that now." Then, seeing Sara's determined expression, she shrugged. "All right—but I just know the bare bones of these stories. You'll have to ask Piers if you want details. He has quite a library on it. Or Julius, although he knows more about ... other things." She hurried on before Sara could question her. "The story is pure superstition. In past times, mole paws were believed to be so much like human hands that they could cure bodily pains if they were placed on the afflicted part. Like easing rheumatism in your shoulder—that sort of thing."

"What does that have to do with me?" Sara asked, knowing her bruises were of another kind.

"There were other superstitions connected with moles, as well. A dried paw is supposed to cure a youngster's troubles when he's teething." Stephanie flushed under Sara's incredulous regard. "I didn't say I *believed* these things."

"Sorry. It's just hard to understand how anyone could swallow such farfetched stuff."

"Throwing salt over your shoulder doesn't rank as logical thinking either—but I'll bet you've done it. And what about dodging black cats?"

"All right. You've made your point," Sara admitted as she took a sip of milk. "But I still can't see what the mole could possibly have to do with me."

"There's another legend," Stephanie said reluctantly. "If the believer wants a person to disappear, he uses the body of a mole to achieve it. Since moles use their paws to burrow underground and out of sight, they're especially symbolic."

"But there weren't any paws left on the carcass. What does that mean?"

"Probably not a darned thing. Piers would have a fit if he could hear this discussion. You'd better go to bed."

"Wait a minute. You say that he knows all about these superstitions?"

Although Sara kept her tone casual, it didn't fool Stephanie. "So do a thousand other people, including me. Julius is full of tall stories, and even Lee and the Colonel could contribute their share."

Sara brushed off her last comment. "Julius..." she said frowning, "You mentioned him before."

Stephanie hovered uneasily in the doorway. "Yes, but this isn't his sort of thing." There was an expectant silence until she tacked on a reluctant admission, "If you *must* know—voodoo is Julius' bag. He'd say that messing around with the paws of a mole was plain crazy."

"Voodoo!" Sara's voice rose. "Good lord ... next you'll be saying that you cast spells in your spare time!"

Amusement crept into Stephanie's pale features. "Only on odd Tuesdays by appointment. Get some sleep now, Sara. By morning, this will all seem like a bad dream."

Sara nodded and watched her close the door softly behind her. As she moved over to deposit her empty glass on the bed table, her mind was still intent on Stephanie's amazing revelations. From the sound of things, Arcady was a hotbed of sorcery and black magic right out of the Middle Ages.

She folded back the bedspread and plumped up her pillow before starting to climb into bed. Then suddenly she hesitated and stripped the blankets back to the footboard. Nothing came into view except an expanse of spotless linen. Feeling more than a little foolish, she replaced the covers carefully before crawling under them.

Once they were under her chin, she resolved to blank out all thoughts of small four-footed creatures and large two-footed males with dark copper hair and outsized egos. Even so, it took a full half hour before she finally fell into a disturbed and restless sleep.

She awoke to the ringing of the phone on the table beside her and was amazed to see daylight streaming around the edge of the curtains as she pushed up on an elbow and reached for the receiver.

"H'lo," she murmured indistinctly.

"Sara?" Stephanie's soft drawl came over the wire. "You sound as if you'd just gotten up."

"I'm not even that far." Sara fumbled to see her travel clock and merely succeeded in knocking it onto the floor. "Darn! Wouldn't you know! What time is it?"

"Almost eleven. Lee says to tell you that he doesn't mind sitting around drinking coffee but that he'll be fired if he doesn't make an appearance at the mill sometime today."

"You mean he's here already?" Sara was horrified. "Good heavens, I forgot to set my alarm."

"Don't panic. I'll tell him you'll be over for breakfast in—"

"Twenty minutes," Sara said, swinging her feet over the side of the bed. "Not a second more."

"All right—your eggs will be ready. Oh, Sara—" Stephanie gave an embarrassed laugh. "I forgot to ask how you felt. Everything's all right, isn't it?"

"Fine, thanks. You can tell that I didn't let anything keep me awake."

"Good! Piers will be glad to hear that."

Stephanie hung up before Sara could ask her what she meant. Thoughtfully she replaced her own receiver, wondering why Piers professed any concern. He had been quick to enlist Stephanie's help last night but only because he was probably ashamed of his own behavior.

Sara's lips tightened as she reached for her robe and headed for the bathroom. At least she wouldn't have to worry about encountering Piers today. Touring the sugar mill with Lee would take the early afternoon and talking business with the Colonel at Bellecourt would fill the rest of the time. Which, she told herself resolutely as she turned on the hot water tap, was exactly the way she wanted it.

The old-fashioned southern breakfast at Arcady deserved a trumpet voluntary, an honor guard, and a royal proclamation.

Sara announced the fact when Stephanie stopped

by her dining room table an hour later. "I have never eaten such wonderful drop biscuits in my life," she confessed. "Or so many. Lee insisted that the only way to eat them was dripping with butter and jam. I lost count after the first half dozen."

"I had trouble getting her to try the grits, though," Lee said from across the table, "but I finally managed to convert her."

"I should hope so." Stephanie signaled to a waitress for more coffee. "What about the homemade sausage? And the eggs? We have our own henhouse here, you know," she announced to Sara.

The latter just sighed. "I finished everything on the plate. With food like that, I'm surprised the Weight Watchers haven't thrown up a picket line at Arcady."

"Don't worry"—Lee leaned over to pat her on the shoulder—"you'll lose all those calories on the mill tour."

"Shall we plan on you for a late lunch?" Stephanie wanted to know.

Sara barely restrained a shudder. "Heavens, no! But thanks anyway," she added hastily. "Lee's arranged to deliver me directly to Bellecourt to meet his father afterward."

"Don't leave it too late if you plan to cover the grounds. The weather report has a storm moving in from the Gulf. Wind and rain . . . and plenty of it."

Sara glanced toward the dining room window. "It's getting overcast but it doesn't look bad."

"Wait and see," Stephanie told her. "Nothing happens in half-measures in Louisiana. The rain comes down in barrels rather than buckets. Sometimes for weeks at a time. And from what Piers said, the roof at Bellecourt has holes big enough for an albatross."

"It wasn't *that* bad," Sara's tone was defensive. "There wasn't any water damage in the master bedroom."

"What's the use of discussing it? You'll be back before the storm breaks," Lee said. He leaned forward to look around the deserted dining room. "Where *is* Piers? I can't understand how he'd miss an opportunity like this."

"He's around." Stephanie's naturally warm drawl was cooler than usual. "Really, Lee, you shouldn't judge everybody by your own instincts."

He laughed and settled back in his chair. "You sound more like a mother hen every day. If this keeps on, he'll have to make an honest woman of you."

Stephanie scraped back her chair and stood up, her normally pale skin mottled with anger. "That's enough, Lee! I just hope that Sara is sensible enough not to listen." She swept out of the dining room, a picture of affronted dignity.

"Oh . . . oh. The lady's lost her sense of humor." Lee felt his jugular vein as if making sure it was still intact. Catching Sara's reproachful glance, he tried to justify his behavior. "God knows why she's so sensitive. She's been dogging Piers' steps for years. The real faithful kind."

Sara lowered her glance to avoid comment. If Lee's mischief was as deliberate as it seemed, it didn't warrant encouragement. Not that she cared anyway, she told herself firmly. Carefully she sought a change of subject. "Stephanie told me last night that you knew something about voodoo. Is that right?"

He sat up straighter. "How in the devil did that come up?" Then, before she could reply, "Julius, I suppose. What's the old fool done now?"

For a second, Sara almost explained about the dead mole hanging on her door. Then she realized that there was no proof to connect the old man with the grisly act. Killing a chicken for dinner—even letting it bleed on a stairway—was a far cry from superstitious nonsense.

"It must have been bad if you can't even talk about it," Lee persisted. "You might as well tell me—nothing's a secret around this place."

"I wish you'd stop putting words in my mouth. It had nothing to do with Julius. I was just curious, that's all." She took a sip of coffee and stifled a yawn. "Sorry. I can't think why I'm still sleepy. I slept like a log last night."

Lee's features eased into a grin. "Never say that around here or you *will* be in trouble."

"What do you mean?"

"Sleeping like a log," he explained. "You wanted to know about voodoo ..." He saw her hesitant nod, "Well, that's one of the expressions with a double meaning. According to legend, witches leave a log in their beds when they go out at night to do their dastardly deeds. That way, no one knows they're gone. When they come back at dawn, they carefully remove the evidence. It's only when they meet another witch that they say 'I slept like a log last night' and waggle their eyebrows. Significantly no doubt."

Sara giggled. "No doubt. Any other tips straight from the cauldron?"

"One or two. If a ghost follows you, sprinkle a little whiskey behind you."

"What happens then?"

"They stop to drink it, naturally. No more ghosts. Simple, eh?"

"Marvelous." She leaned an elbow on the table and rested her chin in her palm. "This is better than household hints. Tell me more."

He looked around before leaning forward and lowering his voice. "There's a magic powder ... it's in pretty short supply but I happen to have a dose or two if you're interested."

She kept her voice as solemn as his. "Oh, I am. Pulverized bats' wings and snakeskins?"

"I didn't ask. All I know is that you put a pinch of the powder in your escort's drink when you're on a date. The results are sensational!" He sat back and resumed his normal tones. "So I'm told."

"Sounds marvelous. What's it called?"

"The Get-Together Powder. What else?"

She burst out laughing. "I'd better stop while I'm ahead. Where did I ever get the idea that voodoo was all shudders and horror?"

"I can't imagine." Lee put his napkin on the table. "Come on, let's get down to the mill or they'll be sending out bloodhounds for me." He took her arm. "Since you're interested, I know of a couple other powders that come highly recommended. I'll tell you about them on the way."

He kept up the steady flow of nonsense during their five-mile trip to the sugar mill, located just south of Bellecourt's boundary line. Lee pointed out the fence dividing the property as his low-slung sports car jounced through the potholes on the mill road.

"I didn't realize that there was any industry so close to the old place," Sara said.

"Dad would have told you when he toured you around later this afternoon. Actually, the mill doesn't detract from the value of your land because the prevailing wind is away from Bellecourt. Any steam or smoke from our chimneys goes toward the river."

"Is there much of that?"

"Not compared to some industries. Pollution is one problem your aunt doesn't have to worry about. She can concentrate on the dry rot in the foundation."

Sara smiled ruefully. "And where she'd get a bank loan for repairs."

"That, too." Lee gestured toward a sprawling plant ahead of them. "Here's where I spend my time. Not much to look at, is it?"

"I didn't know it would be so big." Sara was staring at the complex of buildings which ringed a large muddy lot where cane trucks were clustered, waiting to be unloaded. "Or so noisy," she added as a shrieking whistle pierced the air.

Lee parked beside a one-story building which evidently housed the office staff. "That's nothing. Wait until you get inside the mill. There's nothing dainty about making sugar." He got out and went around to open her door. "Come on, I'll tell you about it as we go."

She hovered beside the car. "Do you want to check in with your office first? I don't mind waiting . . ."

He cast a laconic glance over his shoulder. "Can't be much happening or they'd be out here having fits by now. Let's head for the mill. It's that big building over there." He jerked his head toward the tallest structure whose roofline was dotted with chimneys. A steady stream of forklifts could be seen trundling back and forth between it and a warehouse nearby. "Watch where you're walking," he warned. "This place is full of mud. We all look like pigs by the end of day. Incidentally, how much do you know about sugar refining?"

"Just that it starts out with sugarcane or beets and ends up in five-pound bags at the supermarket. Everything in between is a blur." She smiled disarmingly. "And I should warn you, I get confused when people try to explain anything more complicated than a screwdriver."

Lee bestowed an indulgent look as he pulled up at a weatherbeaten door marked EMPLOYEES ONLY. "In that case, I'd better give you the quick tour."

"Oh, I want to see everything," she assured him earnestly. "It's just that I'm a total loss on mechanical and scientific terms."

"How did you get through school?"

"My only science course was Botany—and I never *did* understand what Mendel's Law had to do with the sex life of a sweet pea."

Lee opened the door and ushered her inside the big plant. "Once the sugarcane gets in here, we have no interest in trivial things like that." He kept her by the wall and waved toward the expanse of equipment honeycombed by metal catwalks alongside the rumbling conveyer belts and mammoth vats. "It's noisy in here," he raised his voice as he bent over her. "First of all, you'll see where the cane comes in on a belt from the outside storage piles. Afterward, it goes past a series of revolving knives to be cut in small pieces. Just follow me and hang on to the railing."

Sara needed no extra warning when they reached the section where wicked-looking blades were mincing the strong cane. She hung onto a metal balustrade and asked Lee, "Do they start taking out the juice at this point?"

He shook his head. "That's the next process. See that series of heavy rollers? First come the crushers ... then the mills. We add water to the crushed cane then to increase the amount of juice extracted."

They walked alongside the slow-moving conveyer belt.

"What happens to the woody part of the cane that's left?" Sara asked. "Do they just throw it away?"

"Lord, no!" Lee was almost shouting as they moved past a six-foot-high bank of creaking steel rollers. "The residue is called bagasse. It's used for fuel, paper, plastics, poultry litter ... most anything you can name." His voice dropped as they crossed over onto another stairway. "Those big cylinders ahead of us are the heaters. The juice goes in there after being strained and limed. Then it's heated to approximately 215 degrees F." He broke into his glib spiel. "Are you still with me?"

"Every inch of the way." She was frowning at the

heaters. "I should think that juice would be pretty dirty."

"You sound like a consumer protective league. Don't worry—the heat and the lime cause the impurities to precipitate. Afterward it goes along here to the clarifiers."

Sara almost stumbled on the grating because she was staring upward at the row of towering metal vats which were supplied by a network of overhead pipes. "If I didn't know better, I could swear this was a distillery."

Lee threw up his hands in mock horror. "This is strictly legal, ma'am." He jerked his head toward the first vat. "We feed the juice in there and those impurities you worried about are allowed to settle. The clear juice at the top goes on out to the evaporators. The muddy stuff at the bottom is sent along to the filters." He led the way to the back of the plant where a workman was reading gauges on a huge metal cylinder. Lee nodded to him and went on to explain. "This machinery changes the juice into two categories: clear and mud." He chuckled at her sudden frown. "Sometimes the mud is called filter cake, if that sounds better."

"I'll take your word for it. What happens then?" she asked with real interest.

"The filter cake goes back out to the fields where it's used as fertilizer. The clear juice is piped on to the evaporator." Lee led her along another catwalk for a few minutes until they came to a complex of machinery looking like a gigantic laboratory with its vats and complicated pipe connections.

"All this needs is a mad scientist running around

in a long white coat stuffing the heroine into the boiling syrup," Sara told him.

"We only let him out nights when the moon is full. Right now we're requisitioning some vestal virgins to go in the cauldrons. If you'd like to volunteer . . ." he paused hopefully.

"I *am* sorry but I already have an appointment for the first full moon," she said. "There's a werewolf living in the apartment above us who plans his get-togethers ages ahead. Last month there was a sit-down orgy for twenty-four."

"Why can't we have neighbors like that?" Lee commented.

"Well, it takes a special talent. There are hardly enough to go around," she assured him solemnly. "Now—about the evaporators . . ."

"Evaporators are damned dull." He kicked the side of one dispassionately before going back to his duties. "It's just as the name suggests—most of the water is removed here and the juice becomes thick and syrupy. Afterward, it goes to the vacuum pans where it's boiled until you get a mixture of sugar crystals and molasses. The last step is the centrifugals," he pointed to a long row of waist-high vats. "We finish with raw sugar or blackstrap molasses. Naturally that's simplifying the process."

Sara stared at a complicated bank of gauges between the vats as they strolled back down a narrow aisle toward the door. "I can see that. Believe me, I'll never take a sugar cube for granted again."

"That's the proper attitude." He glanced toward a glass cubicle and saw a man with a telephone receiver at his ear frantically motioning to him.

"Damn! This is where the problems start. Do you mind waiting in the car? I'll be out just as soon as I can, and it'll be a lot more comfortable than standing around in here."

Sara nodded hastily and then paused in the doorway.

"I'm sorry to bother you for a ride when you're busy. Bellecourt isn't far from here—I can walk."

"Don't be silly." He glanced at his watch. "I'll round up some kind of transport. It's too sultry to walk even a block if you don't have to."

"Well, if you insist. I'll be waiting outside."

There came an impatient rapping of knuckles on the glass behind him. Lee grimaced and said, "Okay, get in the car and I'll sort it out one way or another," before striding toward the summons.

Sara followed his instructions and waited while fifteen minutes ticked past. Finally she stirred and looked at her own watch. It wasn't that she was impatient; the busy scene of the cane unloading nearby would have held her interest for much longer but she was concerned over being late for her appointment with Colonel Sherman. She was wondering if she should find a telephone and call his office to explain, when a young man hurried from the main building and pulled up beside the car.

"Miss Nichols?" He waited for her nod. "Mr. Sherman sent me to drive you to Bellecourt. He's been delayed with some long-distance calls and said he'll get in touch with you at Arcady later on. Okay?"

"Of course," Sara said, relieved that she would make her appointment on time after all. She waited until he had gotten in the car and was driving sedately through the potholes before asking, "Have you worked here long?"

"Over a year, ma'am." He turned onto the main road. "Mr. Sherman said you were just visiting. Are you having a pleasant stay?"

His respectful air made Sara feel as if she were eighty years old and needed help crossing the street. She smothered an impulse to giggle. "Very nice, thank you. I can't get over this marvelous weather."

"It's been good for a spell, but it's about to break. Reckon there's a storm coming in from the Gulf. See those clouds," he pointed to a gray mass on the horizon. "They'll be dumping in an hour or so."

"Maybe I should have brought an umbrella."

"A tarp would be better, ma'am. I've seen it rain so hard that it'll slosh right up offen the highway." The last was delivered in a drawl as thick as syrup in the refinery.

"Then I'd better make sure I'm under cover when the time comes." As they approached the Bellecourt gate, she said, "Don't bother driving in. It's just a short walk up to the house and I'll enjoy it. Be sure and thank Mr. Sherman, will you."

"I'll do that, ma'am. I hope you enjoy your stay." He braked the car, staring for a moment at Bellecourt's impressive facade in the distance. "That's sure a beautiful place—pity it's going to be torn down. Well, I hope you enjoy your stay here." He smiled, nodded shyly, and drove off.

Sara stood looking after him, her forehead creased in a puzzled frown. What in the world had he meant by his comment that Bellecourt was going to be torn down?

She swung round and stared at the old mansion thoughtfully before moving through the gate, which was ajar once again. Of course the boy could simply be taking the plantation's demise for granted. Even a quick look at the place showed that money was the one element that was lacking.

Her steps quickened as she went up the long drive under the canopy of live oaks. Although there wasn't anyone in sight, she decided Colonel Sherman must be close by. The shrubbery and flowerbeds were so overgrown that a regiment could disappear behind the greenery without trying.

A rooster looked up from his scratching long enough to survey her dispassionately before he went back to his search for food. Seeing him reminded her of Julius, and she glanced over her shoulder uneasily. Strange that he wasn't in view. Surely Colonel Sherman would have told him they were coming.

As soon as she approached the front steps, she found her reasoning was right on that score. The old man appeared from the side veranda and greeted her with his usual toothless grin.

"Afternoon, missy. The Colonel said you'd be along. I expected you before this."

Sara had difficulty tearing her gaze from the plump white hen which he had clutched under one arm. The chicken seemed reconciled to its resting place and didn't exhibit any alarm when Julius stroked it with his free hand.

Sara managed a nervous smile, telling herself it was silly to be uneasy near the harmless old man.

LOVE'S MAGIC SPELL

"Where is Colonel Sherman? I thought he'd be waiting; I'm a little late for our appointment."

"He'll be along, missy. What's time to a hog?" At Sara's puzzled stare, he emitted a cracked cackle of laughter. "No offense meant. I've lived alone so long except for a few friends"—he absently stroked the hen's feathers—"that sometimes I forget the right words."

The thought of Julius choosing to live in the antebellum atmosphere of Bellecourt with only a few animals for company made Sara shudder. Suddenly Stephanie's words came back to her, and without thinking of the consequences she said, "Someone told me that you're an expert on voodoo, Julius. Is that right?"

The change that came over the old man's wrinkled features made her wish that she'd had sense enough to keep quiet.

He assumed a belligerent stance, looking like an unfriendly fowl himself, with his neck thrust forward and his head tilted warily. "I don't know who's babbling things like that and telling lies. God knows, miss, I ain't done nothing you need to worry about. Ask anybody round here. They'll tell you Julius knows when to mind his own business."

"I didn't mean that you'd done anything wrong . . ." she began.

He didn't let her finish. "That's right. There's been nothin' wrong. Anybody who says different don't know what he's talking about." In his agitation, Julius' hand went round the hen's neck and it squawked feebly and struggled to escape. "The Colonel can tell you that," Julius went on. "Not many folks'd work for their keep the way I do."

"That's true. I'm sorry you've had a bad time," Sara said, wishing desperately that she could change the subject before he unwittingly throttled the poor hen. "I wasn't casting any aspersions—it's just that I was fascinated by some of the stories I heard. Lee Sherman told me about witches sleeping like a log and sprinkling whiskey on the path for ghosts." She saw the old man's figure relax and took a relieved breath herself. "I suppose it's silly, but I wanted to tell my family when I got back home."

"Why didn't you say so?" Julius' smile split his tanned skin, and when the hen squawked again, he absently deposited her on the ground. "There's lots of stories," he began importantly as he straightened. "Course you can't believe everything. Like folks saying that the crescent moon on outhouse doors is to keep the ghosts away."

Sara kept her tone light. "We don't have many outhouses in our neighborhood at home, but I'll remember. What other stories are there?"

"Well, most women want to hear 'bout love—how to get a man." He glanced at her slyly, pleased by her discomfited look. "It's important that you don't ask for love . . ."

"Oh?" Sara hated herself, but she meekly followed his lead. "What *do* you ask for then?"

"Self-control. It's the living truth," he added hastily. "Women never like to hear it. But most of 'em don't waste any time learning about some stuff that's sure-fire. You mix up a recipe and then put a couple drops right in the middle of your forehead."

He demonstrated faithfully, even to capping his imaginary bottle after completing the charade.

"I don't know why I ask—but what's this wonder tonic called?"

"'Follow Me, Man,'" Julius said solemnly. "There's a shop on Bourbon Street in New Orleans that makes it up, regular-like." He beamed on her as if he'd just imparted the wisdom of the ages. "It never fails."

She couldn't help smiling in response. "I'll remember. Thanks for telling me."

He nodded amiably, half-turning as he heard the sound of footsteps on the side veranda. That'll be the Colonel comin' now. I'd better be movin' along."

Before she could reply, he had hurried around the house out of sight.

Colonel Sherman evidently noticed him disappearing into the shrubbery as well. "So here's where that rascal has been!" he said. There was a determined set to his jaw although he was walking slowly and looked immaculate as usual in a blue-and-white striped seersucker suit worn with a white shirt. "Afternoon, Sara," he added belatedly. "Has Julius been bending your ear long?"

"Not really. Why? Was he missing?"

"Only from the work he's supposed to be doing. Two weeks ago, I told him to lay some drainage tile down by the road. He's done about five minutes work in all this time. And don't tell me that he's an old man," the Colonel added as she opened her mouth to reply. "I've heard it before. Julius has used every excuse in the book. The upshot is that he does exactly what he wants to around here and not one iota more. It's a damn disgrace," he added, fingering some peeling paint distastefully.

Sara felt like saying that if anyone should be concerned with the behavior of a Bellecourt employee, it should be her aunt. Then she decided that such a comment would sound offensive. Beside, the real estate broker obviously had the good of her aunt's property in mind.

"We need that drainage tile, too." Colonel Sherman took out a handkerchief to blot his forehead. "The last time it rained, the land next to the road looked like a bayou. God knows what will happen when this storm hits tonight."

Sara looked up at the threatening clouds. "There isn't any doubt that one's brewing."

"Hardly. It's moving in from the Gulf and it could be a bad one." He gestured toward the trees lining Bellecourt's drive. "Years ago, there were palms as well as oaks along there. But the hurricanes took care of them and the owners didn't bother to replant." He half-turned to shake his head at the mansion behind them. "It's a wonder the house hasn't gone as well. There can't be a decent board left in it. Do you want to look through it ... I understand that Lamont toured you through the other day."

"Yes, he did. We didn't take long, though, so I would like to see it again. If you don't mind," she added.

"Certainly not. I can understand why you'd like a last look." He walked ahead of her to open the door. "Your aunt will undoubtedly want to hear all about the place when you get home."

LOVE'S MAGIC SPELL

Sara nodded slightly. If she had said anything, she would have protested his foregone conclusion that everything had been done to complete the sale except for signing the papers. And yet, if she were to be completely honest, that was just how things stood. There wasn't any reason for her visit now; it was just more sentimental maundering on her part.

She moved through the dim rooms, following the Colonel's lead. He seemed to realize how she felt, for he kept his conversation at a minimum, pointing out some architectural details that Piers overlooked before.

It wasn't until they had reached the second floor that Sara mentioned the remaining furniture. "Piers was telling me about these armoires," she said, going over to stroke the smooth finish on an old cypress piece. "I'll have to ask Aunt Prue if she'd like one."

"Humph," Colonel Sherman snorted as he surveyed the chest, towering a foot over his gray head. "Shouldn't think that it would fit into a city apartment and the freight would cost her a fortune. Hardly worth it," he announced firmly. "Besides all these pieces need refinishing."

"From what Piers said, the value of the chest would more than compensate for the expense."

"That young man should stick to his philandering and stay away from things he doesn't know about."

"What do you mean—philandering?" She was taken aback by his snappishness. "Good heavens, he just guided me through here yesterday. What's wrong with that?"

"You misunderstand me." He started to gesture and then reached for his handkerchief as he saw the dust from the armoire's surface clinging to his fingertips. "I merely made a facetious remark about the young man. Probably because I saw him indulging in a prolonged farewell with an attractive brunette when I left Arcady after lunch on my way here. Certainly there was nothing wrong with the demonstration—except those things should take place in private. Not in the parking lot of a restaurant," he added distastefully. "But I don't know why we're dwelling on *that* subject."

Sara found herself fumbling aimlessly with the catch on her purse. "I don't know, either. Mr. Lamont's behavior doesn't have anything to do with Aunt Prue's furniture."

"Quite right. I was merely questioning Piers' credentials in the antique field. Before you start shipping all that stuff up North"—he waved toward the bed in the master suite—"you'd better check with your family and see if they want it. Otherwise, I can find you a generous offer right here and save you considerable trouble and expense."

"That's very kind of you." Her voice sounded uneven and she wondered why she suddenly felt like crying. At times, she decided, the Colonel stormed over people and their objections like a Gulf hurricane.

"Of course, it's up to you, my dear." He was watching carefully and must have realized he'd gone too far. "And I realize how difficult it is. Having to make such an important decision would be hard at any time. Then when there are emotional complications . . ."

Sara's chin came up quickly. "I can't imagine what

you mean, Colonel Sherman. "Piers Lamont can have a covey of brunettes stationed in the parking lot for all I care. You're letting your imagination run overtime."

"My dear Sara—I wasn't talking about Piers. I meant Bellecourt itself—this old house. There's so much sentiment surrounding it. None of us like to think of its eventual destruction. I certainly wouldn't intrude on any of your personal affairs."

"I'm sorry, Colonel." Sara realized that her protest had made her feelings all too clear—to both of them. She turned blindly toward the upper hall. "There's not much else to see up here, is there?"

He followed slowly. "I don't believe so. Piers showed you the hidden stairway, did he?"

Why did he have to keep harping on Piers, Sara wondered irritably. "I saw the bottom of one on the back veranda," she acknowledged. "Does it come out around here?"

"In this back bedroom." He led the way toward an empty bedchamber, smaller than the rest, whose only furnishing was a marble fireplace along the outer wall. The black marble mantel revealed intricate carving but was marred by a crack on the top. A battered flashlight rested on the end of it along with two candle stubs. "Use that flashlight if you want to do any exploring on the stairway," the Colonel instructed. "Those candles aren't worth a damn. There are too many drafts to keep the flame going."

Sara picked up one of the wax stubs and turned it in her fingers. "Is there some significance to black candles?"

Colonel Sherman pulled on his ear thoughtfully. "Who knows? I don't listen to half the rumors going round this part of the country. You can hear anything you want to."

"But black candles are a sign of bad luck, aren't they?"

"Something like that."

"Or is it something worse?"

"It depends on the mumbo-jumbo." He cleared his throat. "Actually Julius would tell you it's a sign of death."

The candle stub slipped from Sara's nerveless fingers and fell back on the mantel.

"But I wouldn't lose any sleep over it," the Colonel added hastily. "If you start worrying about voodoo curses, you'd never have so much as a deck of cards in the house."

"Why?"

"The Queen of Spades." He shook his head. "Supposed to be a terrible omen. They've got a barrel-full of them to fit every occasion. Like a damn greeting-card rack."

Sara tried to keep her voice casual. "Does voodoo have anything to do with animals . . . small animals?"

"I can't say. The whole thing's a pack of foolishness. Watch out about encouraging Julius with this stuff." He jerked his head toward the candles before adding cryptically, "He's been warned already." Then obviously wanting to change the subject, he ran his hand along the top of the fireplace. "Pity about that mantel. The crack makes it useless for salvage. Otherwise it'd be worth a great deal of money. Take a look at this if you're interested in plantation architecture." He led the way around to the side of the fireplace and pulled on a chain which appeared to regulate the draft. Immediately a section of the paneled wall next to the chimney came ajar as the switch clicked. The Colonel put his shoulder against the wall section to open it farther. "There's no romantic twaddle about this," he said in a matter-of-fact tone. "The house servants had to get the wood to the upper floor and this was the easiest way. The stairway serves this bedroom and the one next to it." He motioned for her to peer over his shoulder while he held the paneled section ajar. "Actually, you don't have to worry about getting caught in there," he added reassuringly. "There's a release catch on the other side."

"I'm not worried." She drew back again. "I peeked up from the ground floor yesterday."

"That entrance should be closed by now." He released his grip on the wall section and watched it settle back in place. "Julius was supposed to have boarded it up weeks ago. It doesn't do any good to lock the doors if every Tom, Dick, and Harry can come up the back stairs." He dusted his fingers again fastidiously. "Well, I think that's about all. Shall we go back to my office and sign the papers?"

"Oh, not so fast, please. I told you—the decision to sell has to be my aunt's."

"I talked to your aunt on the phone yesterday and she informed me that you had her power-of-attorney. Furthermore, she said that she had every confidence in your decision regarding the property."

Sara's lips settled in a thin line, wishing Aunt

Prue had been less enthusiastic in her family loyalties just for once. Of course, it wasn't *her* fault. She had no way of knowing that, for the first time in her life, Sara felt incapable of a quick decision. The sensible thing would be to sign the Colonel's papers and take the next plane north with his check in hand. The offer appeared fair—even generous under the circumstances and yet . . .

"Well?" He tried to sound patient but it was wearing thin. "I *am* a busy man, my dear."

That did it, she decided.

"Then I won't keep you waiting," she said. "I'll need a little longer to think about it and look around. If you want to leave the papers with me . . ."

"I told you," he snapped. "They're at my office."

"Then perhaps you can drop them off at Arcady," she said in a firm tone. "I'll deal with them after *I've* talked to my aunt."

He pushed his handkerchief into his breast pocket with impatient fingers. "When you're looking them over, be sure and note the expiration date of the offer. You don't have much longer to make up your mind, Sara. Of course, you might get other offers, but I doubt if they'll match this one."

"I'll remember." She kept her voice pleasant. "Thank you for showing me around when you're so busy." For a moment she wondered why a small-town real estate broker *was* so busy, and then she forgot about it as he bent over her hand in the courtly fashion he'd shown before.

"It was a pleasure, Sara." The asperity vanished from his manner like dew under a summer sun. "I'll get the papers to you at the Inn. And don't worry,

I'm sure that you'll look after your aunt's interests in the proper fashion. Goodbye, my dear."

He smiled and disappeared down the curving stairway at the front of the house before she remembered that she had calmly dismissed her only transportation back to Arcady. Since she hadn't mentioned it, Colonel Sherman undoubtedly assumed that she'd made arrangements for getting back to the hotel.

She turned toward the veranda. If she hurried, she could lean over the railing and call to him even now. There was no disgrace in admitting the mixup. But her steps were reluctant and finally stopped in the middle of the room.

A ride back to Arcady in the Colonel's car would mean more of his admonitions and probably a detour by his office to pick up the papers. Once he had those in hand, her decision to delay signing would be more difficult than ever.

She shook her head. Darned if she'd meekly give in just because he wanted her to. Then she sagged against the glass door leading to the veranda and sighed. Somehow this day wasn't turning out any better than the previous one.

A glance outside showed that the sun had completely disappeared behind the turbulent gray clouds. At least it should be cooler when she walked back to Arcady, she decided. The prospect of a solitary walk was appealing; at the moment, her thoughts felt as if they'd been stirred roughly with a spoon.

She thrust her hands in her pockets and walked back through the rooms, kicking aimlessly at the dustballs on the wooden floors. Julius must have decided that simple housekeeping was "women's work" and therefore outside his province. It was too bad that Piers wasn't in charge of the old house. He evidently had an abundance of females to care for such things.

For a second, she let herself wonder just who the latest woman was in his entourage. Then, the remembrance of the embrace that she had shared with him the night before made her cheeks flare with color. No wonder Piers was so expert in his lovemaking; he found a different candidate for his attention every day.

She turned abruptly and marched into the back bedroom. There were more important things for her to do than stand around moping.

For one thing, there was just enough time for her to explore the slave stairway before she started walking back to Arcady. After all, it would be fun to mention it to Aunt Prue and see if she remembered it from her childhood.

Sara moved over to the fireplace mantel and picked up the flashlight. She tested the switch carefully before going around to pull the chain which released the paneled wall section. As the metallic click sounded, she smiled with satisfaction. Finally she moved over to pull the partition open far enough so that she could squeeze by.

Then, holding it carefully ajar, she leaned inside just far enough to point the flashlight beam toward a brass chain on the inside wall. She noted with approval that the brass plate behind it gleamed from recent polishing. Evidently Julius found time to keep some things in working order. Since Colonel

LOVE'S MAGIC SPELL

Sherman mentioned that the bottom entrance had just been closed, it stood to reason that Julius had been using the back stairway for his own convenience in past months.

She cast another glance at the inside release chain for final reassurance. The thought of being stuck in that narrow stairwell would be the ultimate in frustration. It wouldn't even be romantic as in the old days when mansions had their priest's holes and hidden rooms for rendezvous. This would merely be uncomfortable and highly embarrassing when the Colonel or Julius finally tracked her down.

Having made certain that she'd taken the necessary precautions, she finally moved on into the stairway. The beam of the flashlight provided ample illumination for the brick cavity when she let the section of paneled wall slip securely into place behind her.

She made her way down the steep steps toward the ground level, letting her fingers trail over the rough homemade bricks which formed the exterior wall. It was a pity there wasn't a family treasure she could try to unearth, but even Aunt Prue had disillusioned her there. "Anything that was convertible to dollar bills or bourbon went out of Bellecourt long ago," she had said flatly.

"No jewels?" Sara asked.

"The good ones disappeared before the silver. I think . . . just *think*, mind you, that there was still a set of garnets around somewhere." She had laughed at Sara's crestfallen expression. "And they weren't very good garnets even then. Sorry, honey— nothing to dig for. Not even green stamps."

Sara smiled as she thought about the flip comment. She could hardly wait to tell Aunt Prue about the magnificent bed and the cypress armoires. Even if she couldn't fit them into her apartment, Sara knew that she wouldn't casually dispose of them to the highest bidder, as Colonel Sherman suggested.

She paused on the third step from the bottom and flashed her light over a sturdy wooden door which today appeared locked in place. Just to make sure, she moved down the last steps and tried the old-fashioned knob. The hardware rattled ineffectually against the bolt.

Satisfied, she turned and climbed back up the stairs, knowing the Colonel would be pleased to find his orders had been obeyed. She paused as she reached the top, breathing more rapidly than usual after the steep steps. This had been a waste of time, after all. Heaven knows what she had expected to accomplish.

Casually she flashed the beam of light along the narrow aperture toward the second bedroom where an outline of light seeped around the panel which boarded up the woodbox.

Her forehead wrinkled as she noted something on the floor by the panel. Then, as she moved forward cautiously to survey it, she saw that it was merely another black candle stub. She rolled it over with the toe of her shoe and wondered how long it had been there. At least long enough to gather a thick coating of dust. Her frown became more pronounced. Julius should take his playthings with him.

Turning, she made her way back to the panel

while she massaged the tight muscles at the nape of her neck with her free hand. How wonderful a cup of coffee would taste right now! Why was it that a person became consumed with thirst when there wasn't anything available? Well, she might as well get used to it—there was still a long walk in front of her before any refreshments were forthcoming. And after the size of the breakfast she had consumed, she didn't need anything to eat or drink for twenty-four hours, at least.

She grinned ruefully, reaching over for the release chain. There was an ominous rustle as the brass plate behind the chain slithered down the brick wall, clattered against the floor, and bounced to rest beside her ankle.

Sara was so surprised that she dropped the flashlight—which crashed down on top of it. Even then, she remembered to hang onto the chain for the release mechanism.

It was only as she bent over to retrieve the weakened flashlight that she knew something was definitely wrong.

Desperately then, she scrabbled for the light and flashed it onto the chain which she was clutching with such determination.

It was a sturdy brass chain which measured fully twelve inches long and it was, at the moment, unconnected to anything except her fist.

Her appalled gaze went back to the gaping hole in the bricks where the chain had been. Then slowly ... inevitably ... it shifted to the movable section of wall, which remained firmly, inexorably, in place.

Chapter Six

Sara's reaction was to sag against the panel and tell it exactly what she thought of it. Her smoldering declaration covered its appalling ancestry, then went on to describe the entire State of Louisiana, its inhabitants in general and herself in particular. Why she had been so weak-minded, so gullible that she hadn't had the sense to even *test* the damn chain before now!

Her mind boggled at her stupidity and only the knowledge that an aching head wouldn't help kept her from thumping the flashlight soundly over the extremity in question. Also, from the looks of the flashlight beam, the bulb wouldn't survive any more rough handling.

Irritably she moved down the narrow passageway, knowing she'd have to retrieve the stub of candle before the flashlight gave up for good. She clamped down hard on her lower lip as she thought about sitting in the dark in the narrow brick passageway waiting for rescue. It wasn't that she had any particular fears of claustrophobia, but it wouldn't help to dwell on it.

At least Colonel Sherman knew where she was.

LOVE'S MAGIC SPELL 143

That thought soothed her as she bent over to pick up the candle. Idly she blew the dust from it while she went over her chances for rescue. There was Lee—if he ever finished his long-distance calls. Or Stephanie when she saw the empty table at dinner. Or even Piers Lamont—if he managed to remember where she fit in his starting lineup.

So there was no need to panic, she told herself. Of course, it wouldn't hurt to go down and hammer on the door at the bottom of the stairway—in case Julius was working nearby.

Ten minutes later, she gave that up as a lost cause. All she had collected was a sore throat from shouting and three splinters in her palm from pounding on the door. A suspicious moisture at her feet made her realize that the threatened rainstorm had started and the deluge was trickling under the poorly fitting door.

Sara's mouth twisted lopsidedly as she trudged back up the stairs. At least she could be thankful that she wasn't getting soaked on her walk back to Arcady. This attempt at positive thought was soured by the knowledge that she'd gladly trudge through a cloudburst if it meant getting out of the damned stairway. She slapped her palm against the brick wall and only succeeded in driving the splinters in farther.

Her shoe hit the brass wall plate which still lay discarded on the floor. She stared down at it irritably, and then, bending over, she picked it up to weigh it in her fingers. It wasn't heavy enough to be of any use. On the other hand, the four corners were hard and sharp . . .

She chewed nervously on her bottom lip and stared at the wall panel. There was no chance there—not a hinge or bolt in evidence. She thought back to the door downstairs and regretfully discarded any hopes there, as well. The sharp brass corners on the switchplate might be able to gouge rotting wood but wouldn't have a chance on recent repairs.

Her glance went down the corridor to the only other escape route: the boarded-over woodbox in the second bedroom. Almost reluctantly she walked toward it while she told herself not to get her hopes up. This, too, would be another exercise in frustration. Nevertheless, her heart was pounding when she finally bent over the panel. It was only about two feet square but it had evidently been there for years, she decided, after the beam of the flashlight showed some rusty nail heads. If she could gouge the wood around them with the sharp brass corners and somehow pry them out . . .

Her heart beat like a triphammer in her ears as she knelt on the floor in front of the barricade. With a packet of matches from her pocket, she lit the candle and dripped enough wax so that it would remain upright on the floor, before extinguishing the flashlight. She'd need that later on if . . . no, *when* she got out, she told herself firmly. Then, with a silent prayer, she started to work.

As the minutes—and then hours—dragged past, there was a continual temptation to abandon the project. The brass plate measuring about three by four inches probably functioned efficiently in its original role, but as a makeshift screwdriver or miniature pickax it left much to be desired. Sara's fingers were soon aching from clutching it. At first, she tried to lift the nails with the sides of the plate, and when that failed, she went at the wood around them, using the brass corners as a gouge.

It was heartbreakingly slow work. The tears streamed down her cheeks when she sank down on the floor to rest and observed the pitifully few shavings that her efforts had generated. The realization that she was in this predicament merely because of her own impulsiveness didn't help.

Irritably, she rubbed away her tears with the back of a grimy hand. It wouldn't do any good to sit there and wallow in self-pity, she told herself. And if she had to sacrifice a few fingernails in her efforts it wouldn't be the end of the world.

Feeling slightly better after that decision, she pushed onto her knees again and picked up the brass plate. Then she bent over the wooden cover and surveyed it closely in the flickering candle flame. As she pressed her hand against an upper corner of the board, there seemed to be a slight movement in response. If she continued to concentrate her efforts there, she might be able to weaken the wooden slab enough to make a hole. Once that was accomplished, she should be able to pry off one side so that she could crawl through.

After that, her progress could be measured with tangible results, but it took three more hours before she had chipped a hole big enough for a handhold. The first time she tried to exert any pressure, the raw edges of the wood bit sharply into her flesh. She winced and instinctively put her scraped palm against her lips, trying to numb the pain. Then, moving more carefully, she wrapped her hand with her handkerchief and started applying pressure to the broken wood again.

It took time, even then. When Sara finally had broken off enough segments so that she could crawl through, her forehead was damp with perspiration and she was shaking with physical exhaustion.

By then she was moving like a determined robot, carefully pushing the flashlight through the hole first, then turning it on and reversing the beam to illuminate her escape route.

The darkness which instantly enveloped her dissipated all caution in her frantic desire to escape. She heard her blouse rip on the wood splinters as she wriggled through the tight hole, but it wasn't until she had reached the other side, lying on her stomach on the bedroom floor and gasping for breath, that she realized she'd scraped the skin along her entire side.

She pushed onto her feet and stood, swaying with tiredness, while she swung the dim beam of the flashlight around the deserted room and tried to get her bearings.

A sudden brightness beyond the windows puzzled her for an instant. Then the drumming of rain on the veranda outside penetrated her muddled senses and her features relaxed. Of course, the storm had broken; it had been raining when she was at the bottom of the staircase, but it seemed so long ago that she had forgotten.

A tremor coursed her body, and she knew she had to get away from the brooding emptiness of that decaying house and into the open air. Even though she was out of the hidden stairway, the walls of the room stretched like prison bars around her, and the sagging floor wavered before her eyes.

She forced herself to cling to the last remnants of her self-control as she stumbled out to the upper hallway and over to the front stairs. She gripped the flashlight in one hand, but her jacket and purse were forgotten as she started down the steps.

At one point, a wood riser started to collapse under her foot, but she clutched the bannister and glided, wraithlike, onto the next step before it gave way.

Anyone seeing her at that moment would have thought that a Bellecourt ghost had risen from the tomb. Sara's hair hung straight on either side of her colorless face and her eyes stared straight ahead as if fixed on an entity beyond mortal comprehension. One sleeve of her grimy blouse had disappeared entirely and her stockings were in ribbons. The rest of her clothes appeared to be clinging only by habit.

Sara was entirely unaware of her appearance as she flung herself at the front door and pulled it ajar. It wasn't until she had floundered out on the veranda steps with the rain pounding down on her skin that a semblance of sanity returned.

She gasped with the sudden chill of the storm and cowered in the shelter of a brick column. The rain was striking the edge of the veranda in a solid sheet, and from the looks of the sodden paths, it had been falling steadily since late afternoon. Overhead, thunder rumbled through the black clouds.

For an instant, she raised her face and let the

drops beat down on her skin. At least she was free! That was the important thing and all she cared about. Better to drown on the path than suffocate in that horrible black stairwell. She glanced over her shoulder and shuddered. All she wanted to do was get away from this place. If she never crossed Bellecourt's threshold again, it would be too soon.

She made her way down the front steps and then hesitated at the bottom, trying to decide which was the best way to go. There was the main path leading to the road ... but probably little chance of getting a lift back to Arcady once she reached it. For the first time, she cast an unhappy glance down at herself. No one in his right mind would give her a lift looking the way she did. That left only Julius for immediate help. There was a slim chance that he would have a telephone in his quarters. If not, he certainly could give her shelter until the storm was over.

Relieved to have found a partial solution to her difficulties, she made her way through the downpour to the path curving around the mansion. Colonel Sherman had mentioned that the caretaker lived somewhere behind the house—surely it couldn't be far away.

The dim beam of her flashlight barely penetrated the black, rainy night, but it did allow her to stay on the path which wound its way through the gardens at the back. A rank, overgrown rhododendron grove made a canopy over the path, breaking the force of the rain. The glossy leaves were a dubious blessing, though, as they were soggy with water which cascaded over Sara each time she touched the foliage.

She had just pushed through the grove and was wondering if she were destined to wander through Bellecourt's gardens for the rest of the night, when she saw a pale flickering of light over to her left.

She murmured with relief and reached up to push her sodden hair from her face. Then, feeling extremely foolish, she tried to wring the bottom of her blouse before using it to blot her face. After that, she quickened her steps, eager to find shelter and hopefully something warm to drink.

The lights grew brighter as she neared the dark outlines of several rundown huts surrounded by a waist-high wall. The buildings themselves appeared to be completely deserted as she approached the barrier and peered over it, wondering where the gate was. Having to climb a four-foot obstacle would be the final indignity.

She frowned and tried to locate the lights she had seen before, realizing that they must have come from a source outside the huts.

An increased downpour made her shudder. This was no time to be standing around without shelter. At least she could follow the curving wall and find the main entrance to the compound.

After a few more steps, she knew she was on the right track. A measured drumbeat sounded through the stormy night with a human chant following the drum's cadence.

Sara froze in her tracks; Julius must have company, she decided. The beat of a triangle and a strident bell had been added to the throbbing drum.

She moved hesitantly forward while crouched in the shadow of the wall. The rain and her personal discomfort were forgotten completely as she saw lights flicker again and found herself staring into a primitive roofed compound with a floor of pounded earth. At the far side of it, Julius was lighting some candle stubs which were pressed into a tree trunk in the form of a rough cross. When he completed lighting the last one, the drumbeat resumed and four men and one woman filed out from the dark interior of the hut. One of the men carried the Congo type tom-tom under his arm as they marched toward the curving wall, while another beat on a triangle, and the third used an iron rod to hammer a flattened metal bell. The remaining man and woman carried a rooster and a hen which were taken to a bench under the elm tree and secured by leather leg thongs. Then, as Sara watched from the shadows, the beat of the music quickened and the column of worshippers re-formed to parade back into the hut. She noticed that they bowed as they passed a gaudily decorated post in the center of the compound with various objects hanging from it. A short leather whip was suspended from one side while immediately above it on the crossbeam was a bright ship model, a long calabash rattle, and a woven tray covered with intricate designs.

Just then, the chanting came again and the woman and men marched out in another formation—two carrying bright flags and the others holding blazing torches. By now, Julius had finished with his candles and stood in front of the elm tree, his bare arms crossed over his chest as he watched the procession. The men carrying torches knelt to ignite a fire that had been smoldering in a shallow dirt pit next to the bench and the chickens.

The flames exploded upward, sending the chickens fluttering and squawking in terror. As if this were the signal for the start of some ceremonies, Julius and his cohorts threw themselves on the ground—their arms stretched out in supplication as their bodies writhed in time to the hypnotic chant. And then as Sara stared in fascinated horror, she saw a long, sinuous body move on the bottom branch of the elm tree and coil its way downward toward the prostrate worshippers below. Flames from the fire pit and the candle cross gleamed against the serpent's skin and he seemed to sway in the same rhythm as the disciples groveling on the ground.

Sara gave a gasp of terror. Suddenly she knew that she couldn't stand to see any more; already it was as if she'd wandered unwittingly into some kind of Purgatory.

Without trying to muffle her footsteps, she turned blindly and fled back toward Bellecourt. Her flashlight was dropped and forgotten as she struggled through the soaking shrubbery whose very branches seemed determined to prevent her escape. She collapsed for a moment against the trunk of an oak tree, trying to get her breath. In that same instant, she heard the sound of heavy footsteps approaching rapidly. Her eyes grew wide as she strained to see through the dark foliage. Until then, the possibility of pursuit hadn't occurred to her, but what if Julius had seen her spying and was coming after her?

She moaned softly and reeled away from the tree. In her panic she ran straight into a clump of Spanish moss hanging from a bottom bough. Instantly her face was covered with its slimy tendrils—like a giant spiderweb trapping her underneath. She struggled backward, but as she opened her lips to scream, a rough hand covered her mouth and she was dragged into the clear.

She writhed under the heavy grasp, using her fists against the intruder's chest as she tried to escape.

"Sara... Sara! God damn it... cut it out!" The terse masculine command didn't begin to penetrate her terror and when she paid no attention, he changed his grip and shook her—hard.

"Oh, please... stop it!" This time it was her voice in a moan of hurt and protest. As the movement ceased abruptly, she peered up into the face bending close. "Piers! Oh, God! You nearly scared me out of my wits."

"I didn't mean to. I thought I'd break my neck trying to catch up with you."

She was only half listening. Instead she was trying ineffectually to remove the moss tendrils from her wet face. "I can't get away from it," she whimpered with desperation. "There must be all sorts of bugs and things crawling in it! Piers, get me out of here or I'll lose my mind. Maybe I have already."

"Don't be a damn fool!" His voice was rough with feeling as he gave her another angry shake. "You're a lot more apt to end up in a pneumonia ward than a nut factory if you don't get out of this storm."

"That's what I was trying to do—get away from the storm, I mean—when I went looking for Julius. And then I found that—" her voice broke off and suddenly her head flopped wearily against his chest.

"I don't even know what I found. I was afraid to stay and see the end of it..."

"Well, forget about it for now," he said, putting a protective arm around her shoulders. "I've got my car parked outside the gates, if it hasn't washed away in this downpour. Can you manage to walk that far? Or at least until we get out of this forest primeval..." His tone was impatient suddenly. "Whatever else he does, Julius damned well doesn't spend any of his extra time gardening."

She started to giggle uncontrollably. "He can't fit it into his schedule. Kill a chicken in the morning, trap a mole in the afternoon, get the sacrifices ready for night..."

"Stop that!" Piers' arm became a band of steel around her shoulders and he pushed her roughly under the oak branches and back onto the overgrown path. "I told you to think about something else." He pulled her close beside him, his grip keeping her upright when she sagged with exhaustion. "Where in the devil have you been all afternoon? Surely not standing outside that peristyle of Julius'."

"I don't even know what a peristyle is." Her voice sounded as lifeless as her body felt. If Piers hadn't been shoring her up, she would have collapsed on the muddy path right then and there.

"That doesn't matter now." Piers was worrying as much about her sudden apathy as her incipient hysteria before. "Where were you, Sara?"

"Locked in the cradle of the deep." It was hard to get the words out because her teeth were starting to chatter.

His grip tightened again. "Make sense, Sara. What are you talking about?"

"You're hurting me." Her protest was instinctive and once his grasp loosened, she was barely able to keep her feet moving. "I can't go so fast . . . I'm so tired."

Piers said something fierce under his breath and bent over her to swing her up in his arms as the shrubbery thinned. "Hold still! We can make better time this way, honey. That's the main gate ahead of us."

The next few minutes were blurred in her mind as she went limp against his rain-jacketed shoulder. She came back to a semblance of reality as she was deposited gently on the wide seat of an automobile. The rain thumping against the roof made the interior sound like a steel-drum band.

"It's noisy but at least you can start to get dry." Piers pulled himself on the end of the seat and slammed the car door behind him. "Now to get you dry and warm," he said briskly. "There wasn't any point in trying before. There should be a blanket somewhere . . ." He was rummaging in the back of the station wagon as he spoke. "Here it is. C'mon, Sara, take off those wet things. Drape this around you in the meantime. When we get back to Arcady, nobody will pay any attention—" He broke off and shot her a worried frown as she remained immobile on the seat. "Are you listening to me?" Then, without waiting for her answer, he pulled her upright and began taking off her ripped and sodden clothes. For all the emotion he displayed, he might have been peeling the leaves from a cabbage. Sara would have protested in ordinary circumstances, but as it was, she was barely capable of moving her limbs in response to his instructions. He took off everything except her nylon underthings and then proceeded to swaddle her in the blanket like an Indian papoose. "That should start to do the trick," he told her grimly as he reached down to shove her loafers back on her feet. "Keep that blanket over your shoulders and up to your chin. Y'hear?"

She nodded faintly. "I ... I ..." She swallowed and tried to stop the chattering of her teeth. Finally she just shook her head and, closing her eyes, leaned back against the seat.

Piers nodded with approval. "That's the girl. Relax ... and I'll have you back at Arcady in two shakes." He opened the car door to transfer to the front seat. "Keep your fingers crossed that the engine'll still start. It would have made more sense if I'd brought a rowboat."

The ride back to the Inn was another blank in Sara's mind. She was only aware of a slight sense of warmth and soft swearing from the front seat when Piers hit a broken patch of pavement hidden under a sheet of water.

"Keep your fingers crossed," he spoke over his shoulder as he reversed the car. "If this gets any deeper, we'll be swimming, and November's hardly the season for skinny-dipping."

The thought of more water, in any form, made Sara shudder. She vowed that nothing other than sheer bodily force would get her out in the deluge again when she heard the engine catch hold after its spasm of coughing and the car crawled forward.

The next thing she knew, Piers had cut the ignition and was opening the car door alongside her.

"We finally made it," he announced tersely. As he saw her blink in confusion, he went on, "Just hang on to that blanket for dear life. I'll carry you straight to your room. Don't worry about seeing anybody—the only things out tonight wear fins or feathers." As he spoke, he was bending over her and hoisting her onto his shoulder. For a second, Sara felt like Cleopatra entering Caesar's court wrapped in a scatter rug, and then as she felt the rain pounding on her head again, the ridiculousness of her reasoning struck her. If Cleopatra had looked as bad as she did, the Egyptian empire wouldn't have lasted a week.

Piers tried to shield her from the worst of the downpour, but they were both dripping by the time he had negotiated the path and reached the porch outside her room. He put her down just long enough to open the door and then unceremoniously bundled her inside. "Stephanie unlocked it earlier when I heard you hadn't come back to the Inn," he explained. "I couldn't reach Lee or his father to find out if they knew anything so I decided to start beating the bushes. Only I didn't think I'd end up doing it literally." As he spoke, he was unzipping his jacket and hanging it on the doorknob. He mopped his face with a handkerchief from the pocket of his cotton slacks and then stood there for a moment, looming large and masculine in the small sitting room.

Her defenseless stare must have disconcerted him because he ran a finger around the top of his navy blue turtleneck, looking ill-at-ease for the first time. Finally he cleared his throat. "You look a little better."

His considering tone made Sara realize that she must have looked bad indeed before. She drew the blanket around her more securely.

"I guess a hot bath's the next thing," he announced. Turning toward the bathroom, he added over his shoulder, "After that, I'll find some food."

He disappeared and Sara shortly heard the water running as he turned on both taps full force. Piers met her in the middle of the dressing room a minute later. "That shouldn't take long," he said, drying his hands. "I made it as hot as you can stand it. Stay in until you're *really* warm." Then, surveying her critically, "Are you sure you can manage by yourself? You still look pretty puny."

Sara's cheeks took on their first tinge of warmth as she remembered how little she had on under the blanket. She moved back instinctively. "I don't need any help, thank you."

His wry grin flickered. "I wasn't offering my services, so you can take that look off your face. Stephanie would help if I call—"

"I'll be perfectly fine," Sara cut into his words hastily. The thought of having to ask the other woman's help for the second night in succession was too much. At least Piers was taking her plight in typical masculine fashion. Probably he was simply relieved that she had reappeared in one piece.

"Well, since you're in such great physical shape, I suggest you get in that bathtub," he drawled, jerking a thumb toward the bathroom door. "And just in case you get any ideas, I'll wait until you're in. Then I'll be back in about fifteen minutes with some food. If you're not out here wrapped up in a warm robe and ready to eat, I'll come in and get you. Understand?"

"Yes, but..."

"I mean it, Sara. You'll be damn lucky to avoid a chill the way things are."

"I know that," she broke in desperately. "I just meant that I don't have a warm robe. I didn't bring one with me." At his disgusted expression, she added defensively. "They take up too much room in a suitcase. Never mind, I can use another blanket."

He shook his head. "No way. I'll bring a robe of mine and leave it outside the bathroom door. Now get going."

Sara got going. She had no choice. The look Piers was bestowing showed that he would brook no opposition. She didn't have the slightest doubt that he would deposit her in the bathtub himself if necessary.

Once she was soaking in the hot, scented water, she wondered why she had even thought of resisting. The chill that had invaded every part of her body gradually seeped away, leaving her exhausted but curiously content. It would be wonderful to stay in that hot water forever. Her eyelids drooped and she leaned her head against the back of the tub.

"Sara! Are you still in there?" The slap of Piers' hand against the wood of the bathroom door sounded like a firecracker exploding.

She sat up in confusion, her heart thudding. "Yes

... yes, of course I'm here. You're early ... it hasn't been fifteen minutes."

"The hell it hasn't. Women!" There was a disgusted mutter and then the door was opened just far enough for him to drop a rust-colored terry robe inside. "Put that on and get out here—pronto. Your soup's getting cold." The door remained ajar for a scant inch. "You're all right, aren't you?" The inquiry was brusque.

"I told you—I'm perfectly all right." As if he cared, Sara thought irritably when she got out of the tub and marched over to close the door. She would have lingered over drying herself but the thought of the hot soup outside outweighed even her stubborn desire to thwart Piers' orders. When she slipped into the outsized robe, she discovered that he'd taken no chances, even tucking her slippers in the pockets.

He was standing in the dressing room as she emerged. As he stared, Sara fidgeted, wishing that her hair wasn't hanging limp on her cheeks and that her lipstick hadn't disappeared along with her purse. She wouldn't have believed that her dark tresses merely framed the translucent loveliness of her smooth skin and her eyes were given a sapphire cast by the faint smudge of weariness surrounding the thick lashes. Her lips looked soft and vulnerable despite her attempt to steady them.

Piers grinned then as if amused by her waif-like appearance in the long robe.

His look made her wish she was modeling the flattering sheer caped peignoir in her suitcase instead. "I feel like a fool in this ... tent of yours. Are you sure it's necessary?"

"It's warm, isn't it?" He motioned her into the bedroom. "Stop complaining and get into bed. I've turned on the electric blanket."

Sara smiled slightly and allowed herself to be led. "If you think I'm going to object to that, you're crazy. Now that I'm warm, I intend to stay that way." She pulled up in surprise when she noticed the array of food on the bed table. "How did you manage all that?"

"I made a personal raid on the kitchen. Will you settle for consommé, chicken sandwiches, and coffee?"

"At this point, I'd settle for octopus and buttermilk." She hesitated before getting into bed. "Thanks for your help. You don't have to wait around any longer."

"You're not getting rid of me quite that easily, Miss Nichols." He chuckled and jerked a thumb toward the food. "If you'll notice, there are two sandwiches, two cups of soup . . ."

"In other words, supper for two, with a few strings attached." She matched his laconic tone. "I get the idea."

"Not many strings. If it makes you feel better, I'll turn discreetly toward the wall while you're getting into bed," he told her solemnly, "but that outfit of yours isn't the kind to bring out the ravaging beast in any man. Besides, I'm hungry right now and frankly you can't compete with that chicken sandwich."

Sara climbed into bed without saying another word. Piers waited until she had stacked both pillows behind her before pouring the consommé and handing her a steaming mug.

"Now," he said when he'd filled another mug and was seated in the upholstered chair close by the bedside, "you were going to tell me what brought about this highly suspicious state of affairs."

"You didn't tell me this was a true confessions session."

"When you eat my food, I pick the topics for discussion," he said easily. "More soup?"

"No thanks. I could end up in indentured slavery if I asked for a second helping of anything."

He merely passed her a sandwich. "Don't tell me Colonel Sherman kidnapped you this afternoon. I knew that he works on complaining the way other men work on their golf game but I didn't think he'd started chasing women as well."

"Don't be ridiculous. He left Bellecourt after we'd finished our discussion. I stayed in the house to explore a little more."

His mug of soup stopped in mid-air. "And?"

Sara's eyes dropped to avoid that level glance. "I got caught in that old fuel staircase at the back of the house. Colonel Sherman told me about the release switch but I didn't check it until too late." She looked up sheepishly. "The darned thing fell apart in my hand."

His expected hoot of laughter didn't come. Instead he scowled fiercely and said, "I don't know where the Colonel gets his information but that switch hasn't worked in years. It never mattered because the door at the bottom of the stairway was always kept open."

"He told me that he ordered Julius to board it up for security reasons. Probably it was just a stupid misunderstanding," she added, trying to be fair. "After all, he had no way of knowing that I would go poking around."

"How long were you stuck in there?"

"It seemed like forever. I finally used the switchplate to pry off the cover on the woodbox in that second bedroom." At his ominous silence, she went on hastily. "It wasn't too bad ... I had a flashlight and a candle, but after a while it sort of got on my nerves ..." Her voice broke on the last words despite her efforts to keep it matter-of-fact and she glanced down so that Piers wouldn't see the glint of tears.

"What happened then?" he asked quietly.

"Not much. I finally got out of the house. Then I thought I'd try to stay with Julius until the storm let up a little. I wasn't exactly dressed for walking back to the hotel by then."

"I remember," Piers said. "So you arrived at Julius' place just in time for the beginning of the ceremony?"

"Lord, yes, but if I'd had any idea of what I was getting into, I would never have stirred from the veranda at Bellecourt." Sara met his glance then, her blue eyes dark and disturbed. "Those poor chickens ... and that snake slithering past that cross of candles ... I couldn't believe it was real. But it *was* Julius' show, wasn't it?"

Piers leaned forward to take the plate from her lap and give her a cup of coffee instead. "You know it was. Drink some of this and calm down."

LOVE'S MAGIC SPELL

She went on as if he hadn't spoken. "He seemed like such a nice old man. And so harmless—"

"You don't have any proof that he *isn't* harmless," Piers cut into her words sharply. "Everybody around here knows that he's been dabbling in a kind of voodoo for years. He's been warned, but as far as I know, he's never done anything actually illegal."

Sara's mouth dropped open with astonishment. "Good lord! Isn't voodoo illegal?"

Piers frowned. "You'd have a hell of a time proving anything was illegal about that ceremony tonight. And there's nothing wrong with having a patio designed for a peristyle . . ."

"You used that word before. I don't even know what you're talking about."

"The peristyle is the courtyard adjoining the *Oum'phor*." At her puzzled glance, he went on patiently. "The *Oum'phor* is a square house which is the temple of voodoo. Actually it's from a design used to build the Ark of the Covenant. Moses was even believed to have been initiated into the tradition of voodoo." Piers gave her a slanted grin. "Believe me, Julius may have the proper spirit but that temple of his is strictly the budget model."

"It looked authentic enough to me."

"Yes, but you didn't stay long enough to see what finally happened," Piers pointed out. "They use the peristyle for the mass ceremonies and rituals but they also use it for healing of the sick."

"Good heavens! Don't tell me that you believe in all that?" She stared at him. "Next you'll be telling me you're a convert."

"Nope. I'm too hard-headed. At least that's what my family tells me. But Julius doesn't make any attempt at conversions. His 'friends' are all willing volunteers."

"You make it sound so . . . reasonable. Why didn't you explain this before?"

"Why?" Piers kept his tone dispassionate. "So you could fire the old man straight away? It's too bad that you had to burst into the middle of things tonight . . . I can see where it could be unnerving without an explanation . . ."

"That's big of you," she replied sarcastically. "It was 'unnerving' to find a mole on my door knob, too. Or maybe you've forgotten that?"

"I haven't forgotten anything," he answered just as irritably. There was a moment of silence while he got up to pour himself a cup of coffee and stood by the table drinking it. "Julius wouldn't be fool enough to pull a trick like that. Nobody's making him close up shop now, but there are plenty of people in the Humane Society ready to pounce if they had any real evidence."

"What about that dead chicken on the staircase in Bellecourt yesterday?"

"If I remember rightly, we had Chicken Jambalaya for lunch ourselves when we got back here. The end result was the same for both chickens," he pointed out.

"Next you'll be quoting that old saw about 'people who live in glass houses,' " she said, wrinkling her nose. "And don't tell me I'm being illogical. I'm well aware of it, but I'm so confused by now that I don't know what to think."

"Hey—that reminds me." Piers put his coffee down on the table and went out to the sitting room for a minute. When he came back, he was carrying a manila envelope. "I must be getting foggy myself. They had this at the front desk for you. Colonel Sherman dropped it off earlier this afternoon."

Sara accepted the sealed envelope with a frown and tapped it against her thumb before finally dropping it, still unopened, on the bed table.

"I gather that's a bill of sale for Bellecourt." Piers sounded only mildly interested. "Have you signed already or is the Colonel still panting on the leash?"

Sara's eyebrows went up in rebuke. "You're so darned clairvoyant, I'm surprised you don't know."

"I can make an educated guess—you're still making up your mind."

"Right again." She stirred and thumped at the pillows behind her. "Although I don't know why I'm still dithering. After tonight, I don't care if I ever see that place again!"

"I'm not surprised; it's certainly a normal reaction after what you've been through. But I'm wondering if you haven't been prodded along the way."

"What do you mean by that?"

"Look, Sara .. " Piers shoved his hands deep in his trouser pockets and gave her a level look. "Don't sign those papers yet. Give me a little more time."

"Give *you* time?" She frowned. "You mean you want to buy Bellecourt, too?"

"Not personally." His voice deepened with impatience. "Let me have until noon tomorrow. By then, I can explain and have a proposition for you to consider. A business proposition," he added deliberately.

She stared back at him, aware suddenly of the distance he was keeping between them. When she thought about it, she realized he hadn't exhibited any personal interest in her since the rescue. Evidently he was still regretting that angry kiss the night before.

She was pleased to find her voice just as cool as his when she replied, "Frankly, it doesn't make sense, but I can wait until noon if you feel it's necessary."

"Thanks."

He didn't sound grateful, she thought. He merely sounded irritable again. Tonight his disposition was reflecting that touch of red in his hair. Or maybe he was tired ... she certainly was. That must be why the talk of business was so depressing.

Evidently her lethargy was catching. Piers rubbed his forehead and said wearily, "If you've had enough to eat, I'll let you get some sleep." A rattle of raindrops against the window made him add, "And don't go running around any more. You'll be lucky if you don't wake up sneezing in the morning as it is."

"It would take a bulldozer to get me out in that rain." Sara pulled the blankets up to reinforce her words. "I've had more than my share, thanks just the same."

Piers nodded. "It wouldn't hurt to make sure your door is locked once I've gone. Tell the desk clerk not to put any calls through until morning and don't answer if anybody comes knocking."

She wilted visibly against the pillow. "*That* does it."

"Does what?" He looked startled.

"If there was anything I didn't need, it's an early

warning system," she told him. "I've been sitting here losing my appetite all by myself. Now you make it official."

"For lord's sake, Sara, just because I don't want you to take any more chances tonight doesn't mean that the roof's going to fall in."

"The bedroom ceiling doesn't bother me at all. I'm terrified that Julius and his friends recognized me. That was supposed to be a secret ceremony, wasn't it?"

"Look, Julius is a harmless old man—there's no need to imagine things."

"Piers—are those ceremonies secret?" she persisted.

"I suppose so." He sounded evasive. "What makes you think they knew you were there?"

"*You* saw me."

"I was looking for you. Julius wasn't."

She wasn't going to be sidetracked. "I must have sounded like a herd of water buffalo when I ran away. That snake crawling down to Julius' shoulder had simply terrified me . . ."

"Look," Piers said reasonably, "you'll have to stop thinking about it or you'll be crawling on the ceiling yourself."

"If you must know—I'm up there now." She took a deep breath. "Piers, you asked me a favor a minute ago—now I'd like to ask one of you."

He stared back at her warily. "What do you have in mind?"

"Could you possibly stay in here with me tonight? I'm sorry to sound like something from the psychiatrist's case file, but it's been an awful day and I'm still petrified with fear. Tomorrow afternoon I'll go back to New Orleans and you can forget all about it. If you like, you can even have this bed—there's plenty of room for me on that couch in the living room." She sat up and started to throw the covers back.

He was beside her in an instant, firmly holding the blanket in place. "Cut it out, will you! I told you I wanted you to stay warm."

"Well, will you do as I asked?" She had trouble keeping her voice steady. "As a special favor?"

He stared down at her, his expression hard to read. "If it would make you feel happier, why not? But I'll bunk down on that couch out there." He jerked a thumb toward the next room. "There's some extra bedding on the shelf in the closet so you don't have to make any more magnanimous gestures."

A faint flush stole over her pale cheeks. "I wasn't about to. Do you want to go back to your room for your things?"

"It isn't necessary. These pants already look as if I'd slept in them and besides, there's no point in compromising you any more than we have to. In case the maids start work early," he added in explanation, "you might be able to explain an overnight guest in slacks and a sweater. But pajamas ..." he shook his head. "Pajamas show definite premeditation. They'd never believe I stayed on the couch."

Her flush deepened. "Your reputation is the one to consider," she pointed out. "After all, you live around here."

"By God, you're right." He kept a solemn face as he drawled, "My mammy warned me about no-count no'thern women. Ah've been searchin' and hopin' to find one all these years."

"Oh, honestly!"

His eyes sparked with laughter as he continued in his normal tones. "It's a damn shame that we're both too tired to do anything about it."

Which couldn't put things more plainly, Sara decided. "I hope that couch isn't too uncomfortable," she said aloud.

"No problem." He gave her a careful look. "I'll leave this door ajar. Sing out if you want anything."

"Thanks, I will," Sara lied, knowing that she'd perish first. He'd find indifference worked both ways.

He bestowed a jerky nod and pulled the door partially closed behind him.

When she leaned over to turn off her bed lamp a few minutes later, she saw there was still a glimmer of light from the living room. She heard the sound of muffled footsteps when Piers assembled his pillow and blanket on the couch. Then the snap of a switch plunged the room into darkness just before a creak of springs came from the ancient divan.

Sara's conscience gave a twinge at that ... it was enough that he had humored her fears without having to suffer an uncomfortable night as well.

Her lips quirked in sympathy as she thought about it, but it was nice to be able to relax finally ... to know that she was safe after all the terrible things that had happened. And she knew instinctively that Piers was too fine a person to harbor grudges. Maybe she could make it up to him some way. She was still smiling softly when exhaustion overtook her and she fell soundly asleep.

But it turned out that the events of the day were not to be dismissed in such summary fashion. Some hours later, Sara's subconscious mind took her back to that dark stairway at Bellecourt. Only this time her attempt to escape was more harrowing, as Julius and his robed disciples filed up the dark stairs searching for her. She heard the sound of their relentless advancing footsteps echoing up the black corridor, the throb of that tom-tom drum, and the disturbing rattle of the calabash gourd. Desperately she tried to shut out the ominous beat, the wailing, chanting voices, but they sounded louder by the second. She had just realized that there was no escape from her prison when she saw the serpent slither from the shadows toward her and she fell sobbing and screaming against the locked panel door.

"Sara ... stop it!" Gentle hands were pulling her up, keeping a firm grip on her bare shoulders as she tried to get away. "Cut it out, honey! You've been dreaming." It was Piers' voice, she decided, wondering why he was at Bellecourt, too.

Her eyelids fluttered in the darkness. "Piers? We have to get away ... they're coming." She struggled to get the words out.

"Shh ... close your eyes. Everything's all right," he whispered. Then she felt a soft kiss at the corner of her mouth before she was pulled into a warm, comforting embrace. Strong arms pressed her head down against his chest and her robe was drawn aside far enough for another light kiss to be dropped on silken skin.

"Go back to sleep, my darling. Nothing will hurt

you while I'm here." He barely breathed the words as he bent his head over hers.

Sara's eyelids drooped but her lips drifted down his cheek and lingered there before sleep eventually claimed her.

Chapter Seven

When Sara opened her eyes the next time, she found that morning had arrived and that the storm had disappeared during the night, leaving a full measure of sunshine as its legacy.

A glance at her travel alarm showed that it was almost ten thirty. She sat up hastily, pulling the robe in place and trying to smooth her tousled hair. Then she remembered it was Piers' robe she had on, and the events of the previous night came flooding back.

She frowned and rubbed her forehead as she tried to sort out the exact sequence. With the bright morning sunshine streaming around the flowered chintz draperies, there was a sense of unreality about everything of the night before. The panicky hours at Bellecourt ... the bizarre ceremony with Julius in the courtyard ... even that panic-stricken dash through the grounds before Piers finally caught up with her.

Piers! Good lord, she'd forgotten that he had spent the night in the other room.

She got up and hurried over to open the door. She stared from the threshold at a davenport which looked blessedly normal except for a pillow and neatly folded blanket at one end. Then she noticed a note resting on top of the pillow and scurried, barefoot, across the room to see what it said.

Piers had been brief and to the point. "See you in my room at noon. Stephanie will show you the way."

He hadn't even bothered to sign it. Sara chewed thoughtfully on the edge of her lip as she read it again. Probably he was just being discreet in case a maid discovered it first. And then she spoiled her logic by deciding it wouldn't have hurt him to be a little more personal.

After all, he had shown more warmth last night. She frowned and leaned against the back of the davenport, trying to remember how much warmth there had been. Certainly nothing until the middle of the night and then ...

An annoyed frown creased her forehead. What had happened then? There was a session of dreams and nightmares so vivid that Hollywood could have used them for an epic. But most of the tableau she remembered was imagination. Or was it wishful thinking?

She glanced at the note again. "Stephanie will show you the way," he'd said. The words hardly indicated undying love. It was more like a note left by the Fuller Brush Man.

Sara slowly walked toward the shower, wondering if her lethargy was the result of yesterday's escapades. As she turned on the faucet she was still telling herself that fatigue and mental depression were the natural result of a lack of sleep and had nothing to do with a six-foot southerner who avoided romantic entanglements like most people avoided the plague.

She stepped under the warm water and pulled the shower curtain around the edge of the tub. There was only one thing to do ... snap out of it ... stop acting like a medieval Guinevere before Lancelot came along. Anybody would think she was in love with the man!

Sara blinked at the bar of soap in her hand as if she suddenly discovered she was clutching a live grenade. Carefully she put it back in the soap dish. She leaned against the wall and let the shower cascade over her, hoping the deluge might wash away her disturbing thoughts if she stayed there long enough.

The water had run cold before she decided that such therapy wasn't helping a bit!

She was feeling better by the time she'd dried her half-frozen form and gotten dressed. She chose a flattering coral-and-white linen print and added a dab of Chanel 19 as further insurance to prove how invulnerable she was. Piers need never know that on this particular skirmish, the South had defeated the North without a shot being fired.

Sara picked up the envelope that Colonel Sherman had left and tucked it under her arm along with her purse before locking the door and making her way to the dining room.

A smiling waitress looked disappointed when she turned down the country breakfast after being seated at a damask-covered table near the door.

"I'm not hungry this morning," Sara told her quite truthfully. "Just toast and coffee, please."

"If you're sure, miss." The woman put her order pad back in her pocket. "Plain coffee or chickory coffee?"

"Plain ... I guess." Sara watched her disappear into the kitchen and come back with a steaming coffee pot.

The waitress filled her cup and then brought a cream pitcher from the neighboring table. "Your toast will be right along. The cook's making some fresh."

"Thank you." Sara took a sip of the hot liquid and almost gasped at its bitter strength. "Oh! I'm sorry," she pushed the cup back, "I think you misunderstood me. I wanted the plain coffee."

The waitress's plump shoulders heaved with laughter. "That *is* the plain coffee, miss. Our chickory is a lot stronger. Maybe I'd better bring you a pot of hot water."

"Maybe you'd better," Sara agreed with a sigh, feeling that she had lost on all counts to the Confederate forces.

Stephanie found her as she was finishing her toast. This morning, the older girl had her hair drawn back in a subdued coil but her royal blue shirtwaist provided a vibrant foil for its beauty. Stephanie seemed entirely unaware of her appearance, however, as she hovered beside Sara.

"Piers was worried about you." She frowned as she surveyed the meager array of breakfast dishes. "And you haven't eaten anything!"

"I've had plenty, thanks." Sara managed a faint smile. "You should market that chickory coffee for an extra energy source. Who needs Arab oil?"

Stephanie grinned back. "Once you get used to it, you'll never settle for less. Piers is back in his room now so any time you're ready . . ."

Sara dropped her napkin on the table and gathered up her things. "That sounds like a royal command. Why all the formality suddenly?"

Stephanie didn't respond to her flippancy. "Bellecourt is a serious business for a lot of people down here." She led the way out of the dining room and past the gift shop on the square toward the guest wing. "Piers knows how we feel. Since he had some time off between jobs, he agreed to help us on the project."

"You make it sound as if I like having to dispose of the place." Sara was hurrying to keep up with Stephanie's pace. "I don't . . . but Aunt Prue simply can't afford to restore it. I've *told* everyone time and time again." Her tone became defensive. "Besides, it's a little late in the day for Colonel Sherman to be complaining about selling the place. He agreed that it needed a fortune spent on it."

Stephanie drew up in front of a door at the end of a corridor. "I wasn't talking about the Colonel." She knocked briskly before going on to explain. "The estate is just an egg for an omelette to him. He'd put his grandmother in chains if it helped his income . . ." Her voice trailed off as Piers, looking immaculate in a light gray suit, opened the door. Stephanie waved Sara in and followed on her heels. "I was just telling Sara here about Colonel Sherman's 'loyalty' to the cause."

For all the welcome Piers exhibited, Sara decided he could be greeting a protest committee from the beet sugar industry. She sighed and let her gaze wander around the room while she tried to subdue the thudding in her breast caused by his appearance. She noted with wry amusement that Stephanie had allotted him a room considerably more luxurious than the average. Beige grasscloth covered the walls with the same shade echoed in opaque satin draperies. A contemporary black-and-brown print covered a long sofa, which evidently converted to a bed at night, and two smaller upholstered chairs. A walnut kneehole desk with a leather picture frame on one corner of it stood against the opposite wall.

"Sit down, Sara. How are you feeling today?"

She looked up, startled, to find Piers beside her with Stephanie already settled in a chair and lighting a cigarette. Hastily, Sara sat down on the divan. "I'm fine, thank you. A good night's sleep was all I needed."

Piers' eyebrows went up as if he were amused about something, but he kept his tone impassive as he said, "I take it that you're still free to discuss Bellecourt's disposition? You haven't signed anything?"

Sara laid the manila envelope down on the arm of the sofa beside her and matched his tone. "That's right. I *did* promise—if you'll remember . . ."

"I haven't forgotten . . . anything, Sara." His mouth softened. "I just wanted to make sure."

"Well, frankly I can't believe our luck," Stephanie said. "I thought the Colonel would have you signed, sealed, and delivered by now."

"Cut it out, Stephanie. Give Sara a chance to hear our side of the story without a sales talk." Piers shoved his hands in his pockets and went over to lean on the desk. "She's had enough of that already."

"This gets more mysterious all the time," Sara said. "Keep on and I'll be expecting foreign agents in trenchcoats to waylay me on a street corner. Are you sure we're all talking about the sale of Bellecourt?"

"Absolutely," Piers cut in. "Maybe I'd better start at the beginning. Stephanie here"—his glance rested affectionately on the other girl— "and her friends in the Historic Preservation Society have been keeping a watching brief on Bellecourt for years."

Stephanie nodded and leaned forward to tell Sara. "You may not know it but Bellecourt is one of the finest mansions in the state—it's a gorgeous example of Greek Revival. And, as far as we know, one of the few Gallier homes in existence. It's a jewel."

"I know." Sara threw out her hands helplessly. "Look, we've been over all this. Just because Aunt Prue can't afford to restore the mansion doesn't mean she's advocating its destruction. Maybe Colonel Sherman can afford to restore the old place eventually. It won't matter if it sits for a few more years. Right now, all he's going to touch is the surrounding property. He needs the additional cane acreage."

"In a pig's eye, he does." Stephanie tapped a finger on the arm of her chair for emphasis. "He won't even be able to take care of the land he has in another month. Lee is pulling out and moving to New Orleans."

"He didn't say anything about it to me . . ." Sara began.

"Nor to me either," Stephanie said. "But his fianceé did . . . when she called yesterday to invite me to their engagement party two weeks from now. Lee's going to work for her family's firm. Very hush-hush." She added with a smile, "She's only telling half the town ahead of time."

Piers was watching the play of emotions pass over Sara's delicate features. He was pleased to see disbelief and astonishment but nothing deeper. When she finally glanced at him for confirmation, he said, "I heard about it, too . . . from my sister. Lee has been going with the girl for a long time. We saw them that night at the hotel. Remember?"

Sara nodded slowly before turning back to Stephanie. "But what does this have to do with me? I've just known him for a few days."

"All of us have been wondering why the Colonel wants any more cane acreage. Especially now—if Lee won't be around to help run the mill and watch over things for him."

Piers spoke up. "Everybody around here knows that the Shermans haven't been using all the land they own for some time. Lee simply wasn't that interested in farming. So when we heard that Colonel Sherman was angling to buy Bellecourt to add to his acreage, it didn't make sense. As an investment, yes—but nothing else."

Stephanie broke in. "And when the news got around that Colonel Sherman had made two recent business trips to New York, right after taking over as resident agent for your aunt, the fat was really in the fire. Most of us wondered what kind of shenanigans he was up to this time, especially after he'd had his wrists slapped by the real estate board a year or so back."

"Somebody could have told me—" Sara began only to have Piers interrupt.

"And condemn the man on hearsay?" He shook his head. "Hardly. As a matter of fact, he hasn't done anything wrong on this sale. The offer he's given is perfectly legitimate and backed by money in the bank."

"Well, then, what's all the fuss?"

Piers held up his hand. "There's one small discrepancy. He has no intention of keeping the property, no matter what he told you. He's acting as agent for a foreign chemical company which needs a Gulf plant for the American market. They've made no bones about wanting to locate around here. When you consider Bellecourt in terms of industrial use, the picture changes. The land runs down to the river at the back of the estate, insuring cheap transportation and direct traffic from the Gulf. Add a central marketing area plus plenty of skilled labor and you'll get the true perspective. There are lots of other companies who've located on the Mississippi for exactly the same reason."

"And it's great for Louisiana's economy so we're not complaining because we're against progress," Stephanie said. "But those sites didn't mean the destruction of one of the loveliest plantation houses in the entire country."

Piers smiled faintly. "The thought of anybody destroying a stick of the old place has been giving the

LOVE'S MAGIC SPELL

Historic Preservation Society indigestion for the last month."

Stephanie surveyed him darkly. "Don't joke! You were pretty upset yourself when you heard Sara was coming down here to finalize the sale."

Sara smiled. "It's a wonder that I arrived in one piece." Then as she thought about it her smile faded. "You don't mean to say the Society has been behind all my troubles here."

"Good heavens, no! We certainly wouldn't stoop to trying to frighten you away—no matter what we thought," Stephanie cut in indignantly.

"There could be only one culprit for most of it," Piers said. "I went out to see him this morning."

"Julius?" Sara asked reluctantly.

He nodded. "Remember, Sara, the most important thing in his life is staying on at Bellecourt. After I told him the truth today, he couldn't wait to explain his part. Evidently the Colonel swore that the only sure way for him to remain at the plantation was to make sure the 'northern folks' sold the old place. The faster the deal was consummated, the better. Colonel Sherman assured him that he could stay on as caretaker as long as he controlled the place—a nice piece of evasion in itself. He also 'suggested' Julius do a few things to get you to sign the papers and speed you on your way. The old fellow swears that the Colonel asked especially about that broken switch in the hidden stair. He also gave permission for the voodoo ceremony last night. He told Julius that he'd square it with the authorities if anyone saw them and objected. Incidentally, you'll be glad to know those two chickens were still alive and scratching in the courtyard this morning."

Sara gave a reminiscent shudder. "That's something, at least."

"The old man asked me to apologize for him and to say that he'd appreciate a chance to stay on."

Sara looked undecided. "Do you think Julius was responsible for the mole on the doorknob?"

"He claims he's innocent of that and I'm inclined to believe him. I'll bet the Colonel arranged for that little touch himself—he wouldn't find it difficult if the pay-off was adequate," Piers added in a cynical tone.

"Then what was Lee's part in all this?" Sara persisted.

"Nothing very bad there. Colonel Sherman knew how 'persuasive' his son could be. I imagine he was covering all the angles to provide a favorable picture of the Sherman family. Lee couldn't very well object even if he'd wanted to. He'd already hurt the old man by choosing a new job in New Orleans after his marriage. I imagine he was delighted to cooperate in entertaining you. From what I saw at the end of the evening," Piers added dryly, "he certainly wasn't finding it any hardship." His expression grew amused at Sara's sudden upsurge of color. Then he went on in a more businesslike tone. "That's about it for the background. Now, if you're still interested in selling the old place, Stephanie has a proposition."

"Honestly, Piers! You make me sound as if I should be standing on a street corner or loitering on a pier in New Orleans," Stephanie complained, but her pale blue eyes were shining with laughter. "Actually I'm so thrilled about it I can hardly talk. Thanks to a generous benefactor who just offered yesterday, the Historical Society can more than match Colonel Sherman's figure for Bellecourt." She named a price that made Sara's eyebrows go up. "I'm authorized to say that the Society will be responsible for the restoration of the entire estate. Within a year, we hope to reopen the house as a museum, and within five years, we should have enough in our treasury to offer Bellecourt to the National Trust for their permanent property. Then we'll finally know the place has been preserved for posterity."

"That sounds awfully good—" Sara began.

"Hey, wait a minute . . . not so fast," Piers cut in. "I know for a fact that Colonel Sherman will raise his ante if he has the chance. Maybe you'd better discuss it with him first."

Stephanie shook her head woefully. "For heaven's sake, Piers—whose side are you on?"

"You know damned well, but I refuse to try and stampede anybody with the Colonel's tactics."

"It's all right," Sara told them, "there are some decisions that are easy to make, and an offer like yours that will preserve Bellecourt is definitely the right one." She smiled. "Even northerners have their weaker moments. You can count on a sizable donation from us to help in the restoration." The smile became shy as her glance wandered to Piers. "So you can see congratulations are in order, after all! The South *will* rise again."

He gave a reluctant chuckle. "Damned if I didn't underestimate you, Sara. Is that a hope of yours . . . or a promise?"

Despite his assurance, she would've sworn that her comment had shaken him. She lowered her lashes. "I don't know—the expression just came to my mind. I must have heard it somewhere recently."

"Evidently." The corner of his mouth slanted upward. "Too bad you can't remember where."

His tone made her wish she could remember when she'd heard those words. Piers must have said them himself last night. She was sure of that. Her eyes met his again in sudden suspicion and she went fiery red at the devilment in his glance.

"Would you two mind clueing me in on the conversation?" Stephanie complained. "Either I need a hearing aid or I missed some dialogue."

"Forget it. Family joke." Piers had regained his calm. He rummaged in the desk drawer and pulled out a legal document. "If Sara's serious about agreeing to the sale, maybe she'll sign this." He handed it to Stephanie who nodded and then handed it on. "It merely gives the Historical Society first option for the property. The final papers will be sent to your aunt in Chicago, so there's no need to delay you if you want to get back home," he added.

Sara stared at the fine print in front of her but her mind was whirling after his casual summing-up. Why didn't he just say, "Here's your hat—what's your hurry?"

She dug into her purse for her pen and was proud of the way she kept her fingers steady when she scrawled a signature at the bottom of the paper. "There you are." She gave the document to Stephanie and stood up. "If that's all, I'll go back to my room and start packing."

"Whatever for? There's not *that* big a hurry," Stephanie said, clutching the document like a cherished child. "I can barely believe this yet! If you'll wait a little while, I'll go call the Society's lawyer. He should be able to give us a closing date for the transaction ... and your aunt will want to know. I'll phone from my office." She hurried toward the door, saying over her shoulder to Piers, "And I'll tell them to send down a bottle of champagne ... for a little *lagniappe*. This is worth celebrating!" The door closed with an ecstatic bang behind her.

Piers had an amused expression on his face. "Stephanie and her *lagniappes*."

Sara nodded with resignation, "Something extra. Really, I wish she wouldn't bother. I can't stay." She moved toward the door, but when she got there she found Piers calmly blocking her escape.

"My dear Sara," he sounded exasperated, "there's no need to start running again. You act like a moving target most of the time. Now go back and sit down. We have a lot to talk about."

"I wish you'd make up your mind," she flared, forgetting her pride. "Two minutes ago you were practically shipping me air-freight to Chicago."

"The hell I was." He took her firmly by the elbow and led her away from the door. "You're imagining things again. If you'll give me a chance, I'd like to exorcise some of your memories. Who knows? You might become so captivated by Louisiana that you'd want to stay here. Never go north again." He stopped by the desk and let his finger trace a path from the soft hollow of her throat up to her chin.

He took his time about it. "What do you think, Sara honey?"

His whimsical tenderness took the last bit of stiffening out of Sara's knees and she clung to the desk for support, hoping that Piers wouldn't hear the way her heart was thundering. "I didn't know you represented the New Orleans Chamber of Commerce in your spare time."

"All the civic groups." His intent gaze moved down to her lips as he drawled, "I can recommend the climate, give you a rundown on the food, and introduce you to some wonderful people."

"It sounds interesting," she admitted. Then, as he moved closer, she panicked and jerked backward, tumbling the picture frame to the rug. "Oh, heavens! I'm sorry."

"No problem." Piers bent down and handed it back to her. "Incidentally, that's our 'generous benefactor' that Stephanie was talking about. She doesn't look like the antique mansion type, does she?"

Sara found herself staring down at the portrait of a lovely brunette with a warm smile. Her glance moved to the inscription in a bottom corner. "For Piers—all my love, Tessa."

Sara swallowed. "She's quite lovely."

"It's a pretty good likeness. Too bad you couldn't have met her when she stopped by yesterday, but it's a good thing she came running when I called." Piers took the picture from her and put it back on the desk.

His casual comment sent Sara's dreams tumbling

like a stack of cards. "You mean you asked her for the money? Just came flat out and asked her?"

He shrugged. "Why not? She can afford it."

"My lord, you don't stop at anything, do you!" Sara's eyes smoldered with anger. "First it's Stephanie, hanging on your arm in the morning. Then, at noon, you switch channels and fleece the nearest brunette out of a fortune because 'she can afford it.' I'm glad that you found time to thank her properly in the parking lot after lunch. The Colonel told me about that—but even he didn't know about your next target."

Piers' face looked as if it had been chipped from the side of Mount Rushmore. "And who the hell was that?"

"Me, of course," she snapped. "The biggest idiot on your list. Practically falling in your arms all over the state. Even begging you to spend the night with me . . . that was the funniest of all." Her voice slurred with emotion. "Why didn't you schedule a replay? One more rescue and you could've had Bellecourt for free. That's the usual payoff, isn't it? Was that how she . . ." her eyes drifted toward the picture frame, but suddenly Piers was shaking her like a terrier after a rat.

"That's enough! One more word and I swear you won't be able to sit down for a week!" His voice flicked over her like a bullwhip, leaving her raw from its sting. "And you're lucky—you almost got the back of my hand. I've never hit a woman yet but damned if you aren't asking for it." Breathing hard, he stepped back, raking her with a contemptuous glance. Then he strode over to the door, opened it, and looked back with his hand on the knob. "Go back to Chicago, Miss Nichols. When you get there, shove that mind of yours into a tubful of detergent. And if you want to call off the sale of Bellecourt, that can be arranged, too. I still carry a lot of influence with the brunette."

When Stephanie came back to the room ten minutes later, she found Sara sobbing on the davenport like a woman possessed. Hastily she deposited her tray of glasses and an iced bucket of champagne on the desk before kneeling beside the stricken girl. "Sara, stop it! You'll make yourself sick. What in the world is the matter with everybody? I saw Piers leaving the parking lot a minute ago and he nearly took my head off. Now, you . . ." She stared down at Sara's huddled figure. "You look simply terrible," she said frankly. "My God, what happened between you two?"

It took a long time—but eventually Sara told her.

Chapter Eight

The afternoon shadows were lengthening as Sara got out of the Inn's station wagon and nodded her thanks to the driver. She watched the car disappear up the narrow country lane before turning to warily survey the house she'd heard about.

As plantation homes went, it came under the "small villa" category rather than the "ancestral mansion" type. It was unlike the West Indian style of architecture found in many Louisiana homes of the vintage with wide porches and elevated construction. Instead, this structure faithfully followed the Classical manner beloved by the Greek Revivalists in the 1850's.

Sara walked up the deserted drive and let her glance rest appreciatively on the tidy lines of the cypress exterior with its board-and-batten finish. The central portion of the house was two stories high, while on either side, two single-storied wings extended, airplane style. Architectural symmetry at the ground level was enhanced by a row of shuttered, floor-to-ceiling windows opening onto a shady, columned veranda. Behind the house with its rolling expanse of lawn and garden, Sara could see the slow-moving current of the Bayou Teche meandering lazily between wide banks. All the scene needed, she decided, was a hummingbird hovering over the flower border and a white-coated man to serve mint juleps on the terrace.

She fumbled in her purse for a mirror, hoping her nose wasn't too shiny after the hour's ride from Arcady. At least her outfit was uncreased. She glanced critically down at the sapphire blue dress which featured narrow vertical tucks running from shoulder to hipline. Otherwise the design was simplicity itself, depending on fit and fabric for its understated elegance. The outward appearances were the best she could hope for—fortunately the queasiness in her stomach didn't show.

She took a deep breath as she approached the front door with its polished brass knocker and rapped firmly. After an interval, she heard footsteps on the other side. Then the door opened and she found herself facing an older woman wearing a neat black dress.

"Good afternoon." Sara's greeting was so faint that she had to hastily clear her throat before going on. "I wonder if you could help me. I'm doing an article on southern homes and I'm just going to be in this neighborhood for today. Stephanie Paige said that there was an antique glass flycatcher and some particularly fine examples of Millard furniture in the house." She smiled disarmingly. "I wondered if I might see some of those things Miss Paige mentioned."

A frown passed over the older woman's face, but she moved aside and beckoned Sara in. "Generally we just open the house for special occasions, miss. If you'll wait, I'll have to get permission."

"Of course. Perhaps I could speak to the owner..."

"I'll see, miss," was all the other promised before she disappeared through a door leading to the back of the house.

Sara let out a breath of relief. So far, so good. She let her glance go around the small but tastefully decorated entrance hall, admiring the winding walnut staircase on one side of it. Getting bolder, she tiptoed over to peek in the drawing room. A priceless paneled ceiling caught her eye first. Then the fireplace with its black-and-gold Carrara marble mantel under a Louis XVI mirror. A needlework firescreen stood in front of it to protect two Victorian chairs with their red velvet covers. But it was the modest, cut-glass dome resting on a round table near the windows that brought a pleased smile to her lips. Stephanie was right! It was a perfectly beautiful flycatcher!

She was so engrossed in its design that she almost missed hearing the swift footsteps in the hall. But if the meeting was a shock to her, its effect approached "force twelve" on the Beaufort scale for the owner of the house.

He pulled to an abrupt stop in the dining room archway, almost losing his balance on the heavily waxed pine floor with its butterfly pegs.

"You!" said Piers Lamont, once he'd regained his footing. His attempt to recover his composure wasn't quite as successful, especially when rubbing the elbow he'd just cracked on the woodwork. "I might have known."

Sara managed better. "Good afternoon," she said coolly. "I've been admiring your flycatcher."

"So I see." He abandoned the elbow and shoved his hands in the pockets of a pair of cotton slacks which had seen better days. The pants apparently matched his mood. "Martha said she left you in the hall."

Sara didn't budge. "I couldn't resist taking a closer look at your house. Stephanie said it was lovely . . ."

"Stephanie talks too much. Incidentally, it isn't for sale. Wander around if you want to but you'll have to excuse me . . ." From his tone, she had already been discarded.

"Piers. Wait! Please." Her soft entreaty caught him before he'd taken more than a step. Despite his brusqueness, Sara could see that he was unhappy. It showed in his eyes and in the stubborn set of his jaw. Obviously the first move would have to come from her. Piers would never let any woman ride roughshod over him, no matter how convincing her wiles.

She smiled ruefully. "I've come to apologize. I behaved terribly—that doesn't change anything, but I couldn't leave without telling you."

He turned to face her, his expression unfathomable. "Honest to God, Sara. Many more women like you and the female sex would be an endangered species."

"I've said I was sorry." Her voice was soft. "But what you said about Stephanie talking too much isn't true. She's the one who explained things."

"Ummmm—I thought so."

Her head came up quickly. "Well, it's more than you did. How in the dickens could I know that it was a picture of your sister? *You* didn't tell me."

"You didn't give me a chance," he pointed out ruthlessly. "You were too busy painting me as the Casanova of Bourbon Street and all points west. I still think I should have tanned you when I had the chance."

She moved back a prudent step or two. "Well, it's too late now. Stephanie also explained how your family has given her moral support this past year."

Piers shrugged. "It's the least we could do. She had the bad luck to fall in love with a married man whose wife is in a mental institution. The doctors say she'll be there for the rest of her life."

"Stephanie says she'll wait for the rest of her life if she has to."

"I know. It's a darn shame there are religious complications." He reached up to rake his fingers through his hair. "Anyhow, she and Tessa have been friends since their schooldays, so it's no problem for us to rally round."

Sara found herself clutching her purse and made an effort to relax. "Piers, are you sure your sister wants to spend all that money on Bellecourt? You're sure she can afford it?"

"Positive. Her husband practically has a direct wire to Fort Knox. Besides, he's almost as anxious to rebuild Bellecourt as Tessa." Piers' drawl became more evident. "Nothing like converting a northerner now and then to help the cause."

Sara flushed. "You mean—a carpetbag invasion in reverse."

"That's it, exactly." He folded his arms across his chest and leaned against the side of the archway. The distant side of the archway.

So that was the way it was to be. Sara felt a definite sinking of her spirits. Apology accepted but nothing in return. So much for any hopes she might have had. Well, at least he'd never know. She squared her shoulders and took a step forward. "That's all I had to say. The driver from Arcady is going to come back for me. I'd better be out in front."

Piers was watching her from under half-closed lids. "Before you go, you might like to see the rest of the house." He nodded toward a door at the end of the room. "No more flycatchers, but there are some nice pieces in the master bedroom. I thought of donating one of the armoires to Bellecourt. Take a look as long as you're here."

"You mean . . . by myself?"

"Why not? I think you can be trusted."

For an instant she hesitated. She resented the amusement in his voice and battled with her normal instinct to tell him exactly where he could go. Then she shot a covert glance across the room and decided it would be easier to do as he said. Admiring his prized antiques was a small price to pay if she could escape after that.

She turned and made her way to the bedroom, without another word. Aimlessly, she wandered around the sunny premises, paying scant attention to a rosewood canopy bed that any English monarch would covet and two elegant Regency chairs. A faint fragrance of roses came from the porcelain potpourri jar set under a window which overlooked the lawn dotted with live oaks leading down to the waters of the bayou.

It was a beautiful scene, and Sara knew that at this moment, Eden wouldn't look any better. She made an unhappy murmur and turned back to the parlor, aware that her defenses were painfully low. Dangerously low. It was time for her to get away from here—somehow.

She pulled up in the living room doorway, noting that Piers had moved from his archway. Now *he* stood by the table, a lean finger tracing the design on the glass flycatcher. He glanced up and said mockingly, "Won't you come into my parlor ..." When she didn't move, he went on in a thoughtful tone. "I might be persuaded to part with this flycatcher ... if you really wanted it."

Her eyes grew wide. "Oh?"

He nodded. "The only thing is—it's part of a package. Goes with the house ... the bed ..."

Sara's heart was thudding so fast that she had to hold onto the door. "I see," she whispered. "It sounds expensive ... how much?"

He named a figure that made her swallow. "It was restored by a very expensive architect," he added apologetically, "but if you're interested, I could toss in a *lagniappe*."

"Something extra?" She could hardly get the question out.

"Me." Then he grinned and held out his arms. "Now get over here, you damned little idiot! I've waited as long as I plan to."

It was a considerable time later that Sara pulled

herself erect on Piers' lap and tried to smooth her hair. They had moved from the parlor to a comfortable contemporary room at the back of the house long before. Piers claimed that the Victorians could make love on horsehair sofas if they wanted but he personally preferred something more yielding.

He put up a hand now and ruffled Sara's hair deliberately before pulling her down to kiss her again in a way that those same Victorians would have deplored. Sara waited an appallingly long time before she started struggling. Then she sat up and tried to put herself in a semblance of order.

"We've got to stop this," she said breathlessly. "Remember, I still have to get back to Chicago . . ."

"Seems an awful waste of time. You could get married here . . ."

"Well, at least I have to tell my family about it," she temporized happily. She leaned forward to trace his eyebrow in a way that could only have one result.

This time, she pushed away almost desperately. "I'm not sure exactly who's the spider and who's the fly," she confessed, "but I'm having a terrible time with the web." She fixed him with a suddenly suspicious glare as he chuckled. "And you were an awful pill to keep me in suspense when I came to apologize. I thought you'd never forgive me."

His eyes glinted with laughter. "If it makes you feel any better, I'd already called about plane reservations later in the week. I didn't think it would hurt if we both simmered down for a day or two."

"I wish I'd known." She dropped her gaze shyly. "I didn't think you cared that much."

His slow smile caressed her. "Honey, I wanted to

make love to you the first time we met. After that, I just needed a little time to get you on my side."

"And you knew darned well that it wouldn't take long," she confessed. "I made that more than evident last night. By the way," she tried to keep her voice casual, "exactly what happened when you came into my bedroom in the middle of the night after I had that nightmare?"

His grin broadened. "From the way you talked later, I thought you knew."

"Everything's a little muddled." She narrowed her eyes as she tried to think. "I must have dreamed some of it."

"You really want to know, huh? What's it worth?"

"Piers!"

When she would've flounced off his lap, she was calmly plucked back to his shoulder again. "Now, my dearest Sara," he went on as if there had been no interruption, turning her head so that her lips were only a whisper away. "If you behave yourself, I might tell you on our wedding night. Not a minute before."

Her skin flushed as those suspicious thoughts of hers crystallized into a certainty. Then the touch of his hands made her shudder with longing and she groped blindly to pull him still closer. "That's blackmail, you beast," she managed to say.

He bent his head to cut off any further discussion. "The hell it is, my love. Just think of it as a little *lagniappe*."

Other SIGNET Romances You'll Enjoy

- ☐ **ONLY COUPLES NEED APPLY by Doris Miles Disney.** Gretchen and Jay—a beautiful young couple anyone would envy. Who would ever suspect the dark bond that united them? Who would believe the sinister schemes that lay beneath their bright surface . . . ? (#Q5953—95¢)

- ☐ **THE SHROUDED WAY by Janet Caird.** A search for sunken treasure and a strange death—and Elizabeth Cranston discovers the key to a mystery which places her love and her life in danger. (#Q5753—95¢)

- ☐ **SECRET HONEYMOON by Peggy Gaddis.** A bride must choose between the man she married and the man suddenly returned from the past. (#P5586—60¢)

- ☐ **DESIRE UNDER THE ROSE (Condensed for Modern Readers) by Perry Lindsay.** A talented New York actress who exchanges her career for a new role as the wife of a Southern millionaire finds that he can give her everything—except the man she loves. (#P5585—60¢)

- ☐ **SYLVIA'S DAUGHTER by Ivy Valdes.** An elderly stranger draws Kate Langley into a tangle of love and hate, scandal and death, and dark family secrets. Could even Philippe—the handsome young man who had captured her heart—free her from this web of bitterness and fear? (#P5584—60¢)

- ☐ **IN SEARCH OF A NAME by Norah Whittle.** Married to a man who was old enough to be her father, Judith Pumphrey yearned for romantic love. Little did she realize that fate would take a hand in reuniting her with Timothy, the man she had once loved. . . . (#P5583—60¢)

- ☐ **INTO THE ARENA by Emma Darby.** A probing novel that searches the hearts of two women in love with the same man. (#C5433—75¢)

THE NEW AMERICAN LIBRARY, INC.,
P.O. Box 999, Bergenfield, New Jersey 07621

Please send me the SIGNET BOOKS I have checked above. I am enclosing $_____(check or money order—no currency or C.O.D.'s). Please include the list price plus 25¢ a copy to cover handling and mailing costs. (Prices and numbers are subject to change without notice.)

Name_____

Address_____

City_____State_____Zip Code_____
Allow at least 3 weeks for delivery

More SIGNET Romances You'll Want to Read

☐ **THE BECKONING DREAM by Evelyn Berckman.** Ann longed to reach out to the man she had fallen so desperately in love with, but another woman prevented her —an unscrupulous woman who knew the secret behind the haunting, recurrent dream that threatened to destroy Ann's life. (#Q5997—95¢)

☐ **WHO IS LUCINDA? by Hermina Black.** Her past was buried in memory. Could she trust this new love that wanted to claim her future? (#Q6247—95¢)

☐ **SECRETS CAN BE FATAL by Monica Heath.** A lovely young girl accompanies a writer to a deserted mansion to work with him on his next book, not realizing that the story he is weaving is the bizarre tale of her own past, a past she has never known (#P5180—60¢)

☐ **HIDDEN CREEK by Katharine Newlin Burt.** A lovely, innocent girl faces heart-pounding danger in her reckless search for love. (#T5966—75¢)

☐ **THE RAINBOW CHASERS (Condensed for Modern Readers) by Marlon Naismith.** When David Lorimer appeared in the village, Louise found herself yearning for his love. But how could she trust her heart to a man whose past was shrouded in mystery . . . ? (#P5621—60¢)

☐ **DANGER IN MONTPARNASSE by Hermina Black.** When a sinister figure from the past suddenly reappeared, Fiona realized with chilling terror that she was being used as a pawn in a perilous charade of love and deception. Would her new-found love, who had rescued her once, be there when she needed him again?
(#Q5877—95¢)

THE NEW AMERICAN LIBRARY, INC.,
P.O. Box 999, Bergenfield, New Jersey 07621

Please send me the SIGNET BOOKS I have checked above. I am enclosing $_____(check or money order—no currency or C.O.D.'s). Please include the list price plus 25¢ a copy to cover handling and mailing costs. (Prices and numbers are subject to change without notice.)

Name_____

Address_____

City_____State_____Zip Code_____
Allow at least 3 weeks for delivery

ASTROLOGY...FOR YOU!
Your Own Personal Computerized Horoscope

reveals...

- **What You Are All About**
- **Your Life Style**
- **Your Success Potential**
- **Your Future... Next 12-Months Forecast!**

The wisdom of Astrology has enlightened people all over the world for over 5,000 years. And... now more than ever. You can share in this knowledge through your own personal computerized horoscope. It tells you more about yourself.

10 Full Pages All About You

SPECIAL OFFER... $8.00 VALUE FOR ONLY $4.00

HOROSCOPE ORDER BLANK (PLEASE PRINT CLEARLY)
INCLUDE $4.00 CHECK OR MONEY ORDER MADE OUT TO: THE NEW AMERICAN LIBRARY

SEND TO: HOROSCOPE OFFER
THE NEW AMERICAN LIBRARY, INC.
P.O. BOX 999, BERGENFIELD, NEW JERSEY 07621

Name_____

Address_____

City_____ State_____ Zip_____

My Date of Birth: Month_____ Day_____ Year_____

My Time of Birth: _____ A.M. / P.M. (circle one)
(If time is unknown, 12 noon will be used)

My Place of Birth: (check one)
☐ Eastern Time Zone ☐ Pacific Time Zone
☐ Central Time Zone ☐ Foreign Country _____
☐ Rocky Mt. Time Zone

Allow 6 weeks for delivery of horoscope. Offer void where prohibited by law. The decision to believe or reject the report is that of the recipient.